Fallout

By
Karlene
Blakemore-Mowle

Best Wishes

Karlene
BM.

xxx

Eternal Press
A division of Damnation Books, LLC.
P.O. Box 3931
Santa Rosa, CA 95402-9998
www.eternalpress.biz

Fallout
by Karlene Blakemore-Mowle

Digital ISBN: 978-1-61572-650-9
Print ISBN: 978-1-61572-651-6

Cover art by: Dawné Dominique
Edited by: Carolyn Crow

Printed in the United States of America
Worldwide Electronic & Digital Rights
1st North American, Australian and UK Print Rights

Thank you to my family and friends who make it possible for me to follow my dreams.

Continued thanks to the wonderful team at Eternal Press for the privilege of making my dreams a reality.

Chapter One

Tully's eyes snapped open in the dark. There it was again. She could hear her breathing, loud in the quiet bedroom, as she listened again for the noise that had woken her.

She swung her legs from beneath the covers, and sat on the side of her bed, awake and alert. The noise came from downstairs, a sound like somebody turning a doorknob—her doorknob! She didn't hesitate. Instinct drove her to creep down the wide carpeted steps that divided the second floor from the foyer, the carpet soft and spongy beneath her bare feet. Through the frosted glass in the center of the front door, she saw the outline of a dark figure, then heard the intruder jiggle the handle violently. Anger spiked her adrenaline.

Easing open the door, which lead to the back of her unit, she felt the salty tang of sea air engulf her senses. Circling around behind the intruder, she paused to allow her anger to fuel her strength as the shadowy figure hunched over the lock on her front door. Without warning, she threw her weight against the dark form, knocking him to the ground in a tackle even her gruff old self-defense instructor would have been impressed by.

He grunted and went face down amid a muffled string of profanities. Tully maneuvered herself until she had her knee planted firmly between the intruder's shoulder blades, his arm twisted in a secure grip across his back, giving her complete control of her victim. Beneath her steady hands she could feel the startled indignation of her would-be burglar.

"Who are you?" she demanded.

"What the hell?" The intruder struggled to twist without success beneath her.

Tully registered his deep voice before repeating her question. "Who. Are. You?"

"Jake Holden," he growled back.

"Why are you breaking into my house?"

"Lady, I have no idea what you're talking about. This is my house. I'm trying to open *my* door."

Now that her eyes had adjusted to the light outside Tully could make out the profile of a strong face, grimacing in pain.

He had short dark hair and was nicely built. Under her knee she noticed his strong neck and broad shoulders. He didn't have the physique of a bodybuilder, all muscle and no neck, but he still appeared to be very fit. She also smelled alcohol. While she wouldn't have said he was inebriated, his reaction time had been off a little.

"I just moved in today. You can check my license and see for yourself," he offered, grunting in pain.

"Where is it?"

"Well, if you let me up I'll get it out for you."

She wasn't about to let this guy up just yet, not until she got to the bottom of this. "Where's your license?"

"Front right hand side in my trousers." His tone came out stiff and full of wounded indignation.

"You've gotta be kidding me. Who keeps their wallet in their front pocket?" she scoffed, thinking he had to be lying to create an opportunity to make a break for it.

"It's not in my wallet. I just took my ID and cash to the pub," he growled, "but if the thought of sticking your hand down my pants scares you—"

"Lie still," Tully commanded, then edged down and slid her hand into his pocket, easing the pressure of her hold just enough for him to be able to lift his hips so she could withdraw the card.

"You know," he commented through tightly clenched teeth, "in any other circumstance I'd find this a complete turn-on."

Ignoring him, she squinted to make out the details written on his license and saw, true to his word, he had recently been down to the RTA and changed his address.

The name on the license was Jake Holden, thirty-eight years old. It listed unit five of her resort-style complex as his address.

She gave a small grunt of irritation. "This is unit four."

She dropped his arm and removed her foot, careful to put enough distance between them in case he tried anything. She tossed the card back at him and, as he rolled over, he caught it one-handed. Good reflexes, considering.

The man lay on the path, rubbing his shoulder as he stared up at her with a thunderous expression. "Did you have to break my arm to point that out?"

"I didn't break it. If I'd wanted to hurt you, I would have."

"Remind me to thank you once I get feeling back in my arm." He eased himself to his feet and leaned back against her door, eyeing her with a good deal of caution.

"You're lucky I didn't call the police," she snapped. "Ever heard of responsible drinking?"

Now that his face wasn't buried in the cement under her foot, Jake could get a good look at her. He'd glimpsed a flash of smooth, tanned skin when she'd released him, and he already knew she was toned. What he hadn't expected was that she didn't look anything like the female weight lifter he'd envisioned.

"I'm not drunk and I only moved in this afternoon. All these damn units look the same in the dark," he grumbled.

She was of medium height; her head would reach his chin, which didn't make her tiny. He figured her to be somewhere around five foot nine or ten. Her short hair looked tousled and sexy and now that his initial surprise had worn off, his curiosity had well and truly spiked. Jake studied her long smooth legs under a nightshirt which barely reached midthigh and saw the outline of her breasts, visible through the thin material of her sleepwear. As she folded her arms defensively across her chest the fabric pulled tight, emphasizing them further.

"Is this how you welcome all your new neighbors?" His voice sounded husky and not as steady as he would have liked.

"Had I known I was about to be awoken by a drunk in the middle of the night, I would have taken time to dress for the occasion," she snapped, then turned and vanished back into the shadows, leaving him to find his own way back to his apartment.

* * * *

The following night, Tully stared up at her ceiling in frustration. She'd ignored the noise coming from next door for three hours, but for the last twenty minutes they'd been playing Cold Chisel songs and belting out the lyrics in typical out-of-key drunken voices...loudly.

At the end of *Khe Sanh* she held her breath. It seemed quiet. *At last!* she thought with a relieved sigh, *they're going to call it a night.* When the opening bars of *Cheap Wine* began, however, she leapt from her bed, dragged on a pair of cut-off denim shorts, and grabbed the small pen flashlight she kept on her bedside table for emergencies. In T-shirt and shorts, she marched down her staircase and through the front door to bang on the door of her new neighbor's unit.

She fumed as she realized they couldn't hear her over the open mic they had running.

As she drew back her fist to bang louder, the door opened, surprising her and catching her mid-strike.

"Whoa there."

A large palm caught her fist before it contacted with the chest of the man who'd opened the door.

"Well, if it isn't Stone Cold Steve Austin," he drawled. "Wrestled any other unsuspecting neighbors lately?"

Tully froze. The hand that still encased hers felt warm and large. His other arm hung by his side, holding a can of beer. If he'd been surprised at almost colliding with a woman's fist as he opened the door, he didn't appear particularly fazed. She took a step backward, tugging her hand free in the process.

"I'm not sure if you realize, but that wall," she said as she pointed past his shoulder into his living room, "divides my place from yours."

His only reaction was to raise an eyebrow as if to say "and?"

Clenching her teeth, she continued with forced politeness. "I finished work at eleven tonight and I have to be back up at six. It's now 2:47...Do you think you can turn the music off and call it a night?"

He considered her request. "Would you like to come in for a drink?"

Her eyes narrowed dangerously. "No, I would not like to come in for a drink. Just turn the damn music down."

"You don't like Cold Chisel?" He took a gulp of his beer and his eyes crinkled. He seemed to take pleasure in aggravating her.

Stay calm. She unclenched her hands by her sides and took a deep breath. "Listen, if we're going to be neighbors it's going to work out a lot better if we can both get on. So you close down this party and I won't have to get nasty. Then everyone will be happy."

"I might like nasty girls. Maybe I'll just take my chances."

The song ended and the sound of male voices, arguing over what song they should play next, carried out into the doorway.

With a tired sigh, she realized she wasn't going to get anywhere with this guy tonight by being reasonable. "Okay, we'll do it your way," she said in mock capitulation.

His amused chuckle followed her retreat into the shadows.

Yeah, laugh it up, pal, she thought as she headed for her target.

The apartment complex was a rather trendy place to live. Double-story duplex units were scattered throughout the development, intertwined with pebbled pathways and well-maintained tropical gardens. It had been a lot more up-market than she'd planned on renting, but had practically fallen into her hands and she'd jumped at the chance to snag it before someone else did.

A quiet person who loved her privacy, having a vacant unit next door had been fantastic. No noisy neighbors, no forced politeness and idle chit-chat to worry about...until now.

Well, if her neighbor wanted trouble, that's what he'd get...

In the dark, she made her way toward the meter box on the side of the unit. She lifted the cover, hearing it squeak in faint protest, then withdrew the small flashlight from her pocket. With it clenched between her teeth, she ran her fingers over the multitude of fuses housed inside. She knew the lecture she'd attended on basic home maintenance would come in handy one day.

Technically, of course, she knew you weren't supposed to mess around with a meter box, but she'd tucked the useful information away in the back of her mind in case of an emergency. Surely, this constituted an emergency? Removing the fuse wouldn't be detected by a cursory, drunken check of the meter box, but would ensure they couldn't flick the power switch and start all over again.

Problem solved.

As she returned to her own unit, she listened to the mayhem breaking out next door. She tucked herself back into bed and waited. The slam of the meter box followed by the rowdy farewells of Jake Holden's partygoers signalled her plan had worked.

With a satisfied smile she drifted off to sleep.

Chapter Two

Tully smiled as she collected a tray of empty coffee cups to clear a vacant table. She wondered what her new neighbor had made of the sudden return of his electricity. On her way to work this morning she'd replaced the fuse she'd confiscated the previous night.

Courtesy of Neanderthal man and his tone-deaf sidekicks, she'd lost a great deal of sleep and the day had dragged. She hated being out of sorts, but it was nothing a good hard run wouldn't fix. Itching to pull on her shoes and feel the natural high of endorphins coursing through her blood, at the end of her shift she changed her work clothes for running pants and T-shirt and headed outside into the shady, fig-lined pathways.

She loved the fact her unit was within walking distance of her day job, and looked forward to the exercise—her way to wake up in the mornings and unwind at the end of her shift. It was also the only part of her old life that she didn't have to give up.

With the sun on her back and a slight breeze whispering past, she closed her eyes in blissful abandon. Noisy seagulls squabbled nearby and the gentle rhythm of waves rushing in and out sounded like the ocean breathing. It was a soothing sound, one that seemed to restore calm within her when nothing else could.

Beneath her jogging gear she'd thrown on her swimsuit, planning a dip in the sparkling blue water of the flat ocean she ran beside. Protected by Magnetic Island, the beaches off Townsville had little wave action, making it ideal for small children and families. Unfortunately, for most of the year you were limited to the places you could swim, using the netted areas to avoid the deadly box jellyfish, or stingers, as they were more commonly referred to as. It seemed such a waste of paradise, to be unable to swim freely, but the risk was far too great to ignore, and the consequences could be lethal.

Feeling refreshed after a brisk swim, she sat on the beach to dry.

Sometimes when she was able to sit and think her mind wandered to thoughts of her future. Where would she be in a year? A year from now seemed a lifetime away. Everything pretty much hinged on one date, which at the moment was six weeks from now, although that could change. Already it had been moved back three times, prolonging the uncertainty of her future.

Scooping a handful of soft white sand in her palm, she let it drizzle to the ground between her feet. There were times when the sheer frustration of having no control over her life became unbearable. Once upon a time she had known exactly where she was going to be one year from now. Nowadays she struggled to keep herself focused on one day at a time.

Tully rose to her feet and dusted the sand from her body, then pulled her clothes on over her now dry swimsuit, to head back home.

Slowing her pace as she neared her apartment unit, she passed a car parked across the road from the complex. Taking note of the license plate she made a sentence of the letters, filing it away in her memory. She watched as it idled past her, feeling a slight niggle of unease before she shook it off and headed across the road.

* * * *

Jake spotted his neighbor as she walked toward him and sent a small salute in greeting. He took in her damp hair and the bronzed glow that radiated from her smooth skin. A sudden jolt low in his stomach made him drop his feet to the ground and sit up straighter. It happened a lot—every time she entered his vicinity. No doubt about it, his neighbor was easy on the eyes, although she seemed oblivious to the fact.

"Been for a swim?"

She stopped but he got the impression she would have preferred to have gone inside without having seen him.

"Yeah, the water was great."

"What kind of job keeps you out so late anyway? Every time I see you, day or night, you're either coming or going to work."

"I work nights down at the 'Bluey'."

"That bar downtown?"

"That's the one," Tully said dryly. "Then days I waitress at a café."

"How many jobs do you actually have?"

"Only two."

"Busy lady."

"Yeah, well someone has to pay taxes to keep all the unemployed fed," she said with a shrug.

He liked the sound of her voice. It had a soft sultry kick that got him every time. "Pull up a pew," he offered, indicating the other chair across the small glass table on his front patio. He saw from the way her eyes dropped that she was about to decline, but then she froze.

His eyes narrowed, taking in the unnatural stillness, and followed her gaze to the newspaper open on the table before him.

"Have you been following it?"

She snatched her attention from the paper to stare at him, puzzled.

Lifting his chin in the direction of the story, he kept his expression neutral.

She shook her head and slid her gaze back to the newspaper. "Not really."

"This guy is some kind of mob boss and the cops have been trying to get something on him for a long time. Seems like the old fella will get off, if what they say in the paper is any indication. Reads like a flaming episode of *The Sopranos*."

"Can't say I've ever watched the show."

Further comment died on his lips as a police car glided into the driveway. His neighbor turned and Jake noticed that her fists tightened by her sides and she shifted her weight to the balls of her feet as though in preparation to flee. Interesting, he thought, as two policemen made their way toward them.

"Morning folks, just doing a routine sweep of the area. After any information residents might have to help us in relation to a spate of break and enters in the district." The policeman in his late forties switched his gaze between the two of them while a younger constable flipped open a notebook ready to record anything of interest.

"Break and enters?" Jake's neighbor's forehead creased into a small frown.

"There's been more than a dozen reported over the last few months. We're hoping someone will remember something that may help us with the investigation."

"Can't say I've noticed anything strange around here. Then again I've only just moved in," Jake offered, leaning forward in his chair.

"What about you, miss?" the senior constable asked.

"You might want to check out a green Holden sedan I've noticed hanging about for the last few days."

"What makes you think this car would be of interest?" he

asked, seeming to assess the woman's face closely.

She shrugged. "Just a hunch."

Jake saw the police officer raise an eyebrow and had to admit, her offhand comment had taken him by surprise too. "Was there anything else about the car that might help us identify it?"

"Would a number plate help?" Her gaze swung to the younger of the men, holding the notebook, and she rattled off the license plate.

The older policeman considered her for a moment before he gave a small nod of his head. "Did you get a look at the driver by any chance?"

"There were two men, both in their early twenties—driver had long dark hair and a tattoo of a snake down his right forearm."

She gave a small irritated sigh as Jake and the two policemen stared at her. "I jog in the morning and I've noticed them sitting in their car on a few different occasions now. Just seems odd. I didn't know about the break and enters, but it might be worth checking them out."

"Some memory you got there," the younger officer murmured.

Again she gave an offhand shrug. "I've always had a thing for numbers. It's just something I seem to remember."

"All right. Well, this might turn out to be very helpful. Thank you for your time." The elder officer sent them a swift nod and signalled to his constable it was time to go.

"Wait." Tully reached down and grabbed the pen Jake had been using to do a crossword earlier. She ripped the corner of the newspaper, scribbling something down as she headed toward the police car in the driveway. "Would you mind giving me a call when you find anything out about these two?"

The officer seemed unable to make up his mind about something. Finally, he nodded. "We'll be in touch, Miss...?" He paused, waiting for her to supply her name.

"Tully...Chambers. Thanks." She smiled and turned to walk toward her unit without another word to Jake.

* * * *

Tully groaned under her breath as she saw Jake outside her front door moments later. She'd tried to ignore the penetrating gaze she'd felt on her as she'd given the police the description of the car she'd seen. He seemed far too perceptive for comfort.

She opened the door but didn't bother with a welcome, waiting for an explanation without comment.

"I thought you might like this," he said, unfolding the newspaper he'd been reading earlier and holding it out, seeming to be watching for her reaction.

She reached out and took the paper, sending him a tight smile hoping to cover her irritation at the interruption. "Thanks, I don't buy the paper much."

"Mind if I come in?"

"As a matter of fact—"

"Humor me. Just for a minute."

Tully weighed up her options here. Chances were if she let him get out whatever it was he seemed determined to say, maybe she could get rid of him quicker. He was proving to be somewhat oblivious to the signs she was not interested in friendly neighbor banter. Stepping back, she opened the door. Confidently, he moved past and left her to follow in his wake. He looked like he'd just gotten out of the shower and smelled so good she was caught off guard at the strange sensation of a man in her apartment.

Stepping around him as they came into the living room she headed for the kitchen. If she was going to deal with this knucklehead, she was going to need caffeine. She dragged out her rusty manners and even rustier social etiquette, to ask if he wanted a coffee.

"Sure. Good thing you remembered that car. Cops probably weren't expecting a break like that."

She spooned instant coffee into two cups and didn't bother to lift her eyes to his face as she went about making their beverage. "Good thing someone was observant then, wasn't it?"

"Freakishly so," he agreed, softening the insult with a slight grin.

"You calling me a freak?" She looked him over as he leaned against her kitchen counter, watching her.

His deep laugh gave her a strange feeling, a warm, tingly kind of sensation, and she turned away as the jug boiled to pour the water into the cups.

"You're pretty observant, for a bartender. It's almost as if you've been trained to expect the unexpected," he mused. "I think you should know your talents are wasted on bar work."

Tully fought to keep her voice calm "You got me. My cover as a CIA operative has been blown wide open. How will I ever be able to complete my mission and save the world now?" She passed him a cup and took up a place across from him, resting her hip against the counter. "What is it you do anyway?"

"Up until recently I was in the army. I got out about three months ago and now I'm trying to figure out what to do with the rest of my life." He shrugged.

"What made you leave?"

"I got injured. Decided I'd pushed my luck enough and it was time to get out."

"Oh."

An awkward silence settled between them.

"It wasn't supposed to be a conversation killer," he joked.

Tully's phone buzzed on the counter between them. A quick glance at the number made her heart kick in alarm.

"Sorry, I have to take this." She didn't wait for his answer or give him time to reply as she headed for the glass door leading to her courtyard to answer the call.

Jake moved across the room to take a seat at the small kitchen table while he waited, positioning himself so he had a better view of Tully outside. Tully. Interesting name for an interesting woman.

Jake watched her speak into the mobile, her expression seeming anxious. Tully Chambers intrigued him. The more he dug, the more contradictions he found. He saw her frown deepen as she listened to the caller on the other end of the phone. There seemed to be very little input on her side of the conversation but she was certainly paying attention to whatever was being said.

Taking a sip of his coffee he grimaced. Sugar. Too often in his previous line of work he hadn't had access to the niceties of life like sugar, milk, or even a hot shower for that matter. He soon realized if he wanted to drink something hot, he'd better get used to it straight up. Now he couldn't drink it any other way. Taking his cup back over to the kitchen, he placed it on the counter and started searching for her coffee to make a new cup.

"May as well make yourself at home, old boy," he murmured under his breath. A brief glance out the window told him she was still engrossed in the call and it didn't look like it was about to end any time soon.

He was busy hunting for a spoon when he pulled open the drawer and froze. For a minute he simply stared down at the black object, his mind scrambling for a logical reason for it to be there.

It took a few minutes to get his head around the fact that Tully kept a gun in her kitchen, not something most women did and not just any gun, but a Glock 22, 40 caliber, semiautomatic pistol. Even he, who had until recently lived and worked around weapons, had never left one just lying around his house like this.

Gently he slid the pistol from its holster and pulled the slide back to check it. He clenched his jaw, irritated to discover it was loaded and ready to fire. Popping the magazine catch, the mag slid easily from the handle and he gave it a cursory examination, noting it was full.

Instinct made him glance up and he started slightly as he found her watching him from the doorway, her eyes focused on the weapon, her body tense and alert.

"Tully, why do you keep a gun in your kitchen?" he asked with a calmness he was far from feeling.

"Do you make a habit of going through your neighbors' kitchen drawers?" Her eyes flashed, although her voice was quiet.

He was not imagining the threat of anger that lay beneath her words. "I was looking for a spoon," he justified, beneath her rapidly cooling gaze.

Taking a step closer, she took the gun from his hand and brushed past him. Retrieving the magazine from where he'd set it on the counter, she slammed it home into the handle with practiced ease, expertly checking the chamber before re-holstering the weapon. She shut the drawer with just a fraction more force than was needed.

Holding up his hands before him in a gesture meant to placate, Jake jumped in before she began what he was sure would be another speech about respecting her privacy.

"I wasn't being nosey, but now that we're here I'm really curious as to why you keep a loaded Glock in your kitchen?"

It frustrated him, the lack of respect some people continued to show toward weapons, ignoring the fact that these things were designed to kill. No wonder gun lovers were given such a bad name.

"What part of 'mind your own business' are you a bit fuzzy on, Jake?" she snapped.

"The part," he said, leaning close and ignoring the sweet, alluring scent of her, "where I find my neighbor has a semiautomatic pistol in her house. That bit tends to make me more than a little edgy."

"Well, relax. I have a license for it, and I know how to use it."

"Then you should know better than to leave a loaded gun in a drawer of all places! They're supposed to be kept locked, in an approved cabinet, separate from the ammo."

"Don't lecture me on the law! Who the hell are you to become Mister Civic Duty all of a sudden?" Tully demanded, pushing away from the kitchen counter to stalk past him.

"I'll tell you who I am." He grabbed her arm and ignored her glare as he turned her to face him. "I'm the man who doesn't want to walk in here one day to find my pretty neighbor has blown her brains out by accident." His gaze dropped from her flashing eyes to her chest, which heaved with indignant aggravation.

"I think you better go." Her voice shook a little and he almost hid a smile. It seemed Ms. Chambers was not as indifferent to him as she seemed.

He released her arm slowly and watched as she turned to head toward the front door without waiting to see if he followed. No matter. He could be patient when he chose to be.

As they reached the door he stopped beside her and looked down into somber eyes. "I think you should know I like a challenge."

At once her eyes flared, sparking anew. "I'm not trying to be some kind of challenge and I'm sure as hell not here for your entertainment."

He grinned. Man, she was sexy as hell when she was pissed off. "Have a heart, Tully. I'm still getting the hang of this civilian thing. I've gotta have something to look forward to."

"Get a hobby," she advised with an acid tone, all but pushing him out the door.

Chapter Three

Tully tucked a loose strand of hair behind her ear and wiped her hands on the apron tied around her small waist. Eleven fifteen and things were only just beginning to warm up in the Blue Moon or the "Bluey" as it was more commonly referred to.

The Bluey was now "the" place to be on the weekend thanks to some fresh new management and was incredibly busy on a Saturday night. It was loud and hectic and just the way Tully liked it. Far too busy to be able to stop and chat with the clientele and far too noisy to even attempt a conversation that involved more than a drink order.

While Tully had been new to bar work, other aspects of the job were like second nature. She could spot trouble a mile off and was efficient at heading it off. She got on well with the bouncers at her workplace but rarely socialized with any of the staff. The other females who worked part-time were all young uni students and had little in common with her at thirty-five. She did her job and went home, keeping her distance socially.

Tonight though, it seemed harder than usual to concentrate and she was turning over the reason in her mind. Between orders, she finally came up with the answer. Jake Holden.

She should have noticed someone had moved in next door. Granted, she'd been at work all day, but she should have picked up on some subtle signs that the unit was no longer vacant.

It seemed the hectic work schedule was starting to wear on her, day shifts at the café and nights here. It wasn't as though she wasn't used to long hours, far from it. She'd been accused on more than one occasion of being a workaholic, but that had been a different kind of work.

The small stab of loss still managed to catch her unawares and she forced the memories away quickly.

The simple fact was she needed to be busy. It stopped her going crazy.

She turned and walked back toward the rowdy end of the bar and, sure enough, they were ready for another round of drinks. If being run off her feet was the criteria she had been searching for, she was in the right line of work. For the remainder of her shift, there was little time to think of anything, much less Jake Holden and that suited her just fine.

The next morning, a cool breeze blew through the open window in Tully's bedroom. It whispered gently across one bare thigh which lay above the tangled sheets.

Cheerful bright-colored parrots squabbled and squawked as they fought over the sweet, sappy grevillea blossoms covering a bush beneath the window.

She pulled the pillow off her face and looked at the clock beside her bed.

Sitting up, she brought the small clock closer to her face so she could focus on the digital numbers, then with a yelp, she dropped the clock back on its table and ran for the shower.

Late! She was never late.

Punctuality was something she prided herself on. She had never once let her professional standards slip before today and a tiny quiver of alarm rang inside her. Was she losing her edge faster than she had anticipated?

In less than fifteen minutes she was showered, dressed, and running for the door.

Her new hair length, shorter than she was used to wearing, had been cut in a hassle-free style that she could literally shake after a shower and it was done. The color was a new addition as well. Having never been a blonde before, there were still times when she caught a glimpse of her reflection and thought she was looking at a stranger.

She pulled the front door closed behind her. The air was already heavy and warm, promising another beautiful day in Far North Queensland. The lingering smell of fruit and ocean followed her to the car, but even this could do nothing to improve her mood. Because she overslept, she would now have to forego her run and use the car.

Sliding in behind the wheel of her small hatchback, she turned the key. The click, click sound of the key turning only added to her growing belief that today was going to be one of those days where the entire universe seemed to be conspiring against her.

With her head on the steering wheel, she was in the process of counting to ten when a sharp tap sounded at the window, making her jump.

Jake Holden stood beside the car, his arms folded across his wide chest, wearing a smug smile.

Fantastic, just when she couldn't possibly envision her morning getting any worse, enter Jake Holden. Staring out the front window and stubbornly avoiding his attempt to catch her attention, she gritted her teeth as he tapped once more on her window.

Angrily, she wound the window down. "What?" she snapped without bothering to disguise her irritation.

"I couldn't help but notice you were having car trouble."

"Really? Oh, so that's why it won't start?" she said sarcastically.

"Do you need a hand?" he asked politely, ignoring her sarcasm.

Reaching for her mobile phone, Tully punched in the emergency number for roadside assistance and strummed her fingers impatiently against the steering wheel. "Thanks, but no, I'm calling roadside assistance now."

An earsplitting screech shrilled through her ear, indicating she had no credit and she tossed her phone back into her bag in disgust.

"What about now?" he asked with a straight face but unable to keep the twinkle of amusement from his eyes.

"Do you know anything about cars?" she asked brusquely.

"I know some." He shrugged, leaning casually against the brick pillar that divided their front porch areas, hands tucked snugly under his armpits and looking far too male for her liking.

Biting back her growl of frustration, Tully leaned sideways and pulled the release catch before opening her door and sliding out of the car to lift the hood. Stepping back with her hands on her hips, she looked down into her old car's insides and sighed. Who was she kidding—she had no idea what to do to make it go. "If you could get my car going, it would be really helpful," she finally said, realizing she was going to have to admit defeat.

"Don't go anywhere." He turned to walk away and Tully noticed him moving somewhat stiffly toward his own unit to reverse out a shiny black four-wheel drive.

With nothing to do but wait for him to fix her car, her mind began to wander. Today he wore a black T-shirt that showed off nice well-toned arms and broad shoulders. His skin was tanned and toughened, proof he'd obviously spent a great deal of his life out in the elements. Jake glanced over and sent her a wink.

Tearing her gaze from his, she groaned, torn between embarrassment and anger that he'd caught her studying him. This man was succeeding where no other had before. Tully Chambers *never* got flustered.

Ever.

"Okay, you can try it now," he said, breaking into her thoughts.

Seated behind her steering wheel once more, Tully turned the key and listened as the little hatch spluttered to life. With a sigh of relief she stuck her head out the window as Jake dropped the hood and walked to the driver's door, hunkering down so he was at eye level with her.

"I had the weirdest dream last night," he said with a shake of his head and a ghost of a smile on his lips.

"As much as I'd love to stop and chat about your dreams," she said dryly, "I'm running really late."

With his forearm resting along the frame of her door and his face dangerously close, Tully noticed that his hazel eyes seemed a deeper shade of green and that the left one had flecks of silver running through it. Momentarily she forgot she was running late, and she felt a strange stillness settle upon her as her eyes locked with his. "I've never seen eyes with silver flecks before," she murmured, then quickly dropped her gaze, feeling stupid as a blush crept up her neck and she realized she'd spoken out loud.

"Occupational hazard." He grinned. "Explosives." He shrugged as though that explained everything.

Tully barely registered his answer; she was still scrambling to pull up her defenses and retreat. "I have to go." She pointedly shifted her gaze to his arm and waited for him to move away.

"I'm having a little get-together later tonight...no." He quickly held up a hand to stall her protest. "It's not going to be a late night, I promise. Apparently my fuse box can't cope with late nights," he said, giving Tully a narrowed stare. "Come over, and I'll prove to you I'm not a drunk and that the other night was a very rare occurrence."

"Thanks, but I can't. I'm working tonight," she said with a sigh.

"On a Saturday night? That's gotta suck," he sympathized.

She gave a small shrug and moved to put the car in gear. Slowly, he stepped away from the door.

"Thanks for your help," she said quietly, before reversing down the driveway, fighting the urge to look back in the rearview mirror.

There was no room in her life at this point for any funny business between her and the good-looking neighbor next door. Men were definitely on her "not-to-do" list for a long while yet.

Jake smiled to himself as Tully drove out of sight. He was smart enough to pick up on the definite "back off" signals she was sending out, but something about her overrode his normally well-honed self-preservation skills. The woman did have a gun in her apartment though.

He shook his head as he turned back to look at his unit, grimacing as he pictured the boxes he still had left to unpack. So much for the boys lending a hand the other night. They'd helped him unload the heavier furniture but other than that, not much else got done.

As a rule he rarely drank. In his profession, he had to be ready to deploy at a moment's notice. He'd gotten used to not drinking, but that was now all in the past. He'd left the army.

That simple fact was still raw enough to make him shake his head in disbelief.

He was no longer in the army.

Discipline had been a part of his every waking hour since he had turned eighteen and joined the military. It riled him to have her think he was some party animal, unable to control his drinking. He took his duty seriously and it didn't sit well with him to have his self-control questioned. Come to think of it, it didn't sit well with him to be caught off guard and tossed like a salad by a woman half his own weight either!

Nope, Tully Chambers was certainly not the typical woman he was known to favor. Since coming home, he'd tended to avoid women, but not because he'd lost interest—that thought sent a shiver of horror through him. It was because emotionally, it had taken quite some time before he was able to deal with the horrific burns to his entire torso received during his time in combat.

He tried not to dwell too much on those memories. All things considered, he guessed it was lucky he was still here at all, but there had been days when the pain had been so unrelenting he'd wondered exactly how one defined luck.

It had been a long and painful journey both emotionally and physically to get to this point. It was a gradual transition adjusting to civilian life after leaving the army three months before.

Tully was the first woman who had managed to spark a serious interest in him since he came back. He wasn't sure if that was a good thing or not. To acknowledge that interest would mean he'd have to face the possibility of a woman's revulsion and ultimate rejection when she saw his scars.

Pushing the thoughts away as he usually did when he began thinking about them too much, he decided to deal with it when the time came, if the time came, he corrected himself with a bitter twist of his lips. Judging from the reaction he just received trying to rescue a damsel in distress, it was unlikely he would be getting close enough to Tully Chambers for it to be a concern.

Tully's eyes opened wide in fright. She couldn't breathe. Instinctively her hands were at her throat trying to prise the tightness from around her neck. Sitting up in bed, she stifled a scream and forced deep, rugged breaths into her body. She felt the sweat drenching her nightclothes. After a few moments, the last of the nightmare receded and she realized where she was.

Outside her window blue and red lights flashed, making disco patterns across the walls of her bedroom. Untangling her limbs from the mess of bed clothing, Tully moved silently across the room to observe the drama unfolding in front of the apartment across from her own. People began to float outside in different states of dress. Some wore pajamas, odd mixtures of men's T-shirts and undershirts, skimpy silk shorts and old favorites with their stretched-elastic tops.

A man and woman stood close together, giving information to a uniformed policeman as two other police officers escorted a pair of dark-clothed men from inside one of the apartments. Handcuffed, the men were placed in separate cars and driven away, their progress followed by the inquisitive stares of the growing crowd of onlookers. Gradually the crowd dispersed as the final police vehicle left the scene.

Tully went back to bed and closed her eyes. She'd recognized, in the distance, the barrel-chested policeman who'd been asking questions a few days before and wondered if maybe her information had paid off after all. She hoped so. Two less criminals on the street had to be a good thing.

The insistent buzz of her mobile phone on the bedside table near her head woke her the next morning.

"Miss Chambers, this is Senior Sergeant Malvoy. I'm just letting you know that the information you supplied to us the other day lead to the arrest of two men last night. Seems that gut instinct of yours was spot on."

Sitting on the edge of her bed, she was suddenly wide awake. "Do you know anything about these guys? Are they local? Have they ever done time? Have they any connections interstate?"

There was a pause. "Is there something you'd like to share with me, Miss Chambers? Do you have some kind of connection to these men?"

Tully shut her eyes and tapped the phone against her head, cursing silently at her stupidity before trying again. "No connection. I guess I watch too many crime shows."

The voice on the other end of the phone was still tinged with skepticism when he went on. "I can tell you, since you seem so interested, these two seemed to be working alone and appear to be pretty small-time."

"Thank you, Sergeant, that makes me feel much better." *Much, much better,* she repeated mutely as she disconnected the call and placed the phone back on the table. A little of the weight she'd been carrying on her shoulders, the niggling concern that the men in the car had been something other than small-time criminals, had been put to rest and she felt lighter. She really hadn't wanted to pack up and leave town just yet, and it had nothing to do with her annoying, nosey neighbor, she told the little voice inside that scoffed at her protest.

She decided to forego her morning run, opting instead for the beach. A towel, book, and bottle of sun cream joined her usual necessities in a canvas beach bag and she was headed out the door in record time. She was soon mixing with the tourists and families who frequented the Strand on the weekends. People watching, something she loved to do, done part from habit, was also a very peaceful way to pass some time and relax.

A cry from a seagull nearby drew her attention back to the beach. Tully couldn't help the small sigh of pleasure which escaped as she took in the view. Nature certainly knew how to put on a remarkable display. The sky was a vibrant blue and the ocean flat and smooth before her—she loved how it sparkled a deep shade of sapphire. The lush green palm trees were almost hypnotic as they swayed gently along the foreshore.

She stepped out of her denim skirt and pulled her T-shirt over her head. Beneath, she wore a brown bikini, its halter top sensible and considerably demure compared to some of the younger girls she saw scattered along the beach dressed in barely more than two miniscule triangles and a piece of dental floss. She spread her towel on the warm sand, and lay down on her stomach where she alternated between reading and scanning the area around her. Even in these gorgeous surroundings she found it hard to completely relax. She was about to drop her eyes back to the page in front of her when she caught a familiar face also scanning the area.

Tully watched Jake as he made a casual, yet methodical scan of his surroundings. He was obviously searching for something... or someone and somehow Tully had a pretty good idea who he was looking for.

She made no attempt to attract his attention but waited to see if he would find her. It didn't take long. She knew it was ridiculous but the moment his gaze found her she felt the hairs on her arms raise, as though his gaze had caressed her from a distance.

Pushing away the sensation, she composed herself as he made his way across the beach to where she lay.

"Hey, neighbor," he said as he dropped to the sand beside her, his eyes on the water before them. "You're a hard woman to pin down." His tone was hard to define.

Momentarily, her mind wandered, a vivid picture of him pinning her down made her mentally slap herself. "I wasn't aware I needed to leave anyone an itinerary of my day." She shrugged, trying to hide the small thrill it gave her to realize he had indeed been looking for her in the first place.

A crooked grin touched his lips as he swung his gaze toward her. "You certainly have a sting in your tail, Chambers." She saw his eyes sweep across her body and that odd tingling started again. The soft fabric of his faded T-shirt showed off his arms and broad shoulders to perfection.

She dropped her eyes back to her book without comment and hoped to deter him from further conversation by giving him the silent treatment. After realizing she had read the same line repeatedly, she gave up on trying and closed the book with an impatient sigh. She noticed for the first time since he sat down what he was wearing below the waist.

"Aren't you hot in those long pants?"

Jake gave a small shrug. "I wore a uniform for twenty-odd years. Guess I'm used to it."

"Still, it's got to be almost ninety degrees out here today. You must be hot," she persisted.

"Not really." Something about his tone warned her that the topic was not going to go any further. Tully made a mental note to dig into that a bit later.

"Have you always lived here?" he asked casually.

Too casually. Tully suppressed a groan. She hated when people started to get too nosey. Why couldn't everyone else be like her and mind their own business? *She* didn't strike up random conversations with strangers and expect a complete personal profile on demand. Why then, did everyone else seem to need this?

"I moved here five months ago." *Five months and three days to be exact.* She returned her gaze to the water and watched a large tanker in the distance. A few small craft zipped across the water. Everyone seemed to be out enjoying the glorious weather today.

"What made you move here?" he asked.

"I always wanted to visit and when I did, I didn't want to leave. There are worse places to live." She indicated toward the scenery before them with a nod of her head.

"Why do I get the feeling you really hate talking about yourself?" he asked after a few moments of companionable silence.

"Is it a crime to like to keep your personal business *personal*?" she snapped as she changed position on the towel. "There really isn't anything that interesting about me."

"Now *that,* I find very hard to believe."

Tully suppressed a sigh as she gathered her belongings and rammed them into her bag, before standing to yank on her skirt and T-shirt. So much for the peaceful morning she'd envisioned on the beach. "Well, I'm getting pretty hot out here. I think it's time I headed back home for a swim."

Jake turned and followed her. Together they trudged through the white sand that squeaked and squelched beneath their feet.

"I'm curious about something, Chambers," he announced as they reached the grassed area of the park.

Tully looked over at him skeptically.

"The other day when I was in your place I noticed something odd."

"Besides my gun, you mean."

He chuckled. "Besides your gun. You have almost no furniture, no fancy TV, your car is a bomb. So why do you work yourself into the ground doing two jobs?"

Tully wasn't sure how to answer him. She certainly hadn't expected that. "Maybe I have an expensive shoe fetish and huge credit card bills to pay." She sounded slightly more defensive than she'd intended and cursed silently. This guy was far too sharp to risk allowing herself to react.

"Do you?" he shot back bluntly, completely undeterred by her response.

Was this guy for real? "It's none of your damn business. I don't harass you with all kinds of personal questions, do I?"

He shrugged and took a step closer. "Ask away."

Tully self-consciously tucked a strand of hair back behind her ear and took a step back from him. He was far too unsettling for his own good. "I don't want to know anything."

"You're not the least bit curious about me?" he asked, raising an eyebrow in disbelief.

"Nope."

"Not even a little bit?" He edged a step closer toward her.

"I know enough," she said but watched him warily.

"Like what?"

Like you smell really, really good, she found herself thinking, but pressed her lips together so her thoughts couldn't slip out accidentally. "Like you ask too many damn questions," she muttered, stepping around him.

Jake gave a small, gruff chuckle, dodging a high-speed child on rollerblades and Tully took advantage of his distraction to put some distance between them.

The walk back to the apartments didn't seem to take very long, but Tully felt hot and sticky. The oily residue of her sunscreen lingered on her skin and she could smell the aroma of coconut oil and, strangely, hot chips from the kiosks they passed by on the way home.

Tully stopped by the pool as they entered the apartment complex. "I'm going to take a dip before I go inside." Pulling her shirt over her head, she stepped out of her skirt, slicing neatly into the water to surface moments later, blinking water from her eyes as she smoothed her hair back from her face. Looking up at Jake leaning against the pool fence, she pushed off from the side and floated on her back.

It was almost as though she felt his gaze as he watched her from his position at the fence, and Tully's cheeks reddened as her body responded to his glance as easily as if it had been a caress. Thankfully the coolness of the water against her skin tempered the heat in her response, and she dropped her feet to the floor of the pool and submerged herself underwater. The water lapped her shoulders as she lazily swept the water between her fingers, letting it wash away the heat of the day. "You coming in?"

"Maybe later. Actually, I have a few things I need to take care of...I might catch up with you later." He seemed to trip over his words in his haste to get away. With a brief wave of his hand he backed away from the pool.

Tully stared after him for a moment, then pushed off to swim a half dozen laps of the pool to work off the confused and surprisingly dejected feelings Jake had left in his wake.

* * * *

Later that afternoon she took her dinner outside to enjoy the cool afternoon breeze that the back patio caught in the evenings.

As she munched on her salad sandwich she could hear the occasional grunt and murmured curse from over the fence. After a few minutes she realized Jake must be tackling his overgrown back yard. The unit he had moved into had been vacant for some time and she'd noticed the plants had been on the verge of over-running the yard.

A loud grunt of pain and string of profanities alerted her to the fact that something had gone wrong. Pulling herself up on the fence, she looked over the top. A small chuckle escaped before she could smother it.

Quickly she climbed back down and dragged a chair from her table to the fence. She swung herself over the fence to land lightly on the other side. Dusting off her palms, she walked to Jake's side to inspect the damage. Somehow he'd overbalanced while pruning and stumbled back against a bougainvillea. While its magnificent blood red petals and speckled green foliage were gorgeous to look at, they hid a multitude of savage thorns beneath.

"Stop moving and let me take a look." Her hands skimmed along his back as she tried to unhook his clothing from the plant.

"Damn it, Chambers, what *are you* doing back there?" he growled as she coaxed the prickly plant away from his skin.

"This isn't going to work. You'll have to take your shirt off. I can't get it untangled and you're bleeding."

"I'm fine."

"You're making it worse. Just take off your damned shirt. Here, let me do it." Without waiting for his reply, she walked around to stand in front of him, her hands reaching for the buttons on the front of his shirt.

Slapping her hands away he gave a low rumble. "I'll do it."

Planting her hands on her hips, she indicated with a flounce of her hand it was all his. She held his gaze for a moment, wondering at the almost defiant expression in his eyes and the slight lift of his chin. Impatiently she moved back to stand behind him. "Just slide out of it slowly and I'll unsnag it." Holding the garment as he slipped his arms from it, she gave a satisfied grunt as she freed the shirt from the nasty thorns and turned around to present him with the trophy.

He stood before her, an unmovable, half-naked statue. Tully's gaze dropped from his hooded expression down to his wide chest before lifting to meet his gaze in alarm. Jake had told her he'd been wounded in combat, but she hadn't expected his wounds to be anything like the painful, disfiguring mess she'd just seen covering his chest and back.

Grabbing the shirt from her hands he brushed past her without further comment.

Still shaken, she followed Jake's path through the opened door into his unit. Overhead she could hear the slam of cupboard doors, then heavy footsteps as he made his way down the stairs.

Tully glanced up and held his dark gaze steadily as he made his way toward her. He came to a stop, now dressed in a clean shirt, standing almost toe to toe before her.

"Did you lose your way?"

"You're going to need antiseptic on your scratches." Holding his thunderous expression she sympathized with him. Vulnerability was an emotion she worked hard to avoid.

He gave a short, mocking laugh. "You really think a few scratches are my biggest problem?"

"Bougainvillea thorns can give you a nasty infection if they aren't treated. You won't be able to reach them by yourself."

"They'll be fine, Tully. Just leave it."

"Take off your shirt, Jake." She refused to give him the angry satisfaction of pushing her away.

His eyes flashed. "You weren't appalled enough the first time?"

"For God's sake, Jake, I just want to make sure you're okay."

"I'm not going to slit my wrists if that's what you're worried about." She saw his hands clench as his sarcasm hung thick in the air between them.

He was right. What was she doing? She should leave the guy alone. He was trying to forget an uncomfortable moment and she was going all *"let's talk about it"* on him. He was an adult, a *soldier* for Christ's sake, and she was making a federal case out of... what? Hurt feelings? Damn it, here she was trying to reach out, and he was pushing her away. For goodness sake, the man had been a royal pain in the arse, trying to get her attention all this time and now that he had it, he was throwing it back in her face.

Throwing her hands in the air in frustration, she backed away from him. "Okay, sorry to impose. When you get over feeling sorry for yourself, you know where I am." She let herself out the front door, slamming it for good measure behind her. It felt good to vent her frustration in an impressive exit.

Later that afternoon, the sun was sinking low and the afternoon shadows had begun to fall. A knock sounded on her door and when she opened it, she found Jake standing there, wearing an expression that tugged on her tired, bruised heartstrings.

She stood to one side silently as he entered the house and followed him out to the kitchen. Moving across the room she withdrew a cold beer from the fridge, and a bottle of wine which she poured into a glass for herself. He accepted his beer with a soft "thanks" and sat at the kitchen counter looking down at his can, avoiding her gaze.

"I'm sorry about today. I guess I overreacted a bit," he said without looking up from his can of beer.

Tully took a sip of her wine but remained silent, somehow sensing his need to get things off his chest in his own time.

"I just prefer not to terrify young children and the general public by exposing my body to them. It's not something I feel comfortable with yet."

"I'm sorry that it happened like that. I..." she faltered momentarily, then shook her head. "I had no idea."

He shrugged her apology off, but the dismissal didn't quite reach his eyes, which still seemed heavy with embarrassment and pain. "I can't reach the bloody scratches and they're stinging like a..." He paused, no doubt to prevent what she was sure would be a colorful description. "Would you...put some antiseptic on them... please?" He raised his eyes and in their depths she saw a hollow, haunting darkness.

Her heart squeezed painfully as she realized how hard it must have been for this man to come here and ask this. Maybe she had no right to push him into confronting his injuries the way she had earlier. He, on the other hand, had every right to want her to leave him the hell alone. After all, how would she have reacted in the same position? Tully gave a small wince as she envisioned exactly what she would have done. Remorse filled her anew and she bit her lip uncertainly.

"Look, Jake. I'm sorry if I came across pushy earlier..."

"Forget it." He shrugged, wincing as the action pulled at the freshly torn skin.

"I shouldn't have pushed you about it—"

"I said, forget it, Tully." He cut her off briskly. "Can you just put the damn antiseptic on and be done with it?"

Biting back her apology, she clenched her jaw and gave a stiff nod.

Slowly he stood, and she realized once more just how tall he was up close. She had to lift her gaze a considerable way to meet his.

"I don't want your pity, Tully," he warned in a tense, low voice as he held her gaze intently.

Tully straightened her shoulders, reaching out to take the tube of antiseptic he withdrew from his pocket. "That's good, 'cause I didn't plan on giving you any." She waited while he removed his shirt, and bit the inside of her cheek to keep her emotions neutral, but noticed her hands shook slightly.

Gently, she applied the cream to the deep scratch marks across his back. The skin beneath her fingers was not smooth and tanned like the rest of him, but rough and welted, looking raw and painful even though they'd obviously had many months to repair.

Tully finished tending the scratches, but almost against her better judgement, found herself drawn to the rest of the welted scar tissue lower on his back. She felt his harsh intake of breath at her touch and half expected him to stop her...but he remained motionless as she continued to trace butterfly-like tracks across his skin, silently taking his pain and suffering within her.

Jake stood, frozen in place, and she heard his breathing catch, feeling the violent shiver that went through him. As she circled to stand before him, her movements were slow and deliberate, as though dealing with a distressed animal whose trust she was trying to gain.

It crossed her mind this was pushing the bounds of neighborly conduct. To touch his scars in this way was personal, intimate. There would be no way to return to the distant, aloof relationship she had been trying to maintain before this, but there was an almost magnetic pull that dragged her along in its wake, overriding her common sense and better judgement. It was so completely out of character for her it almost felt like some out-of-body experience...except there was *nothing* remotely out-of-body about the reaction she was experiencing at the moment!

Her gaze wandered across the horrific damage that covered his body. This was his legacy of battle, something that would be a part of him forever more. She reached out and placed her hand above his heart, feeling it thud strongly beneath her palm.

"That's enough." His voice was an anguished whisper, raw, as he caught her hand in a tight grip and removed it. "Just leave it, Tully." He stepped away and broke the potent attraction which had flared all too briefly.

"Jake, I..." She started to apologize. For what, she wasn't sure. The moment had happened too fast. What she had glimpsed, though, was his uncertainty and his fear. He was a proud man who didn't have a great deal of experience dealing with the emotions he kept hidden beneath his tough exterior.

Something she could relate to.

He let himself out the front door, leaving Tully to stare after him, feeling more than a little shaken by the whole encounter.

For a long time after, her emotions were a cocktail of weird and strange combinations. She was mortified he had rejected her sincere attempt to empathize with his pain, but there was also a small amount of relief.

It's a good thing he rejected your offer to...what? Seduce him? How could she do something so out of character? What on earth had she been thinking?

Well, from now on she would keep her distance from Jake Holden. He'd done her a huge favor. Had he not rejected her, she could have been about to make a very big mistake. An attachment—no matter how brief—would only further complicate her life at this point.

Chapter Four

The next week, Tully made sure she asked for extra shifts and was relieved she hadn't even glimpsed her neighbor. Then on Friday of the next week, just when she was sure it was okay to let down her guard, she looked up to find Jake seated at the bar waiting to order.

He watched her, in an attempt to assess her reaction before he ordered a beer. He thanked her as she handed it to him and took his money.

The rush seemed to be over and although it was almost closing time, the last of the patrons seemed reluctant to leave.

Tully had enough to keep busy, as she cleaned and packed things away for the night. She felt Jake's eyes on her and knew he was waiting for a chance to speak with her. Delaying for as long as possible she reluctantly moved toward his end of the bar. "We're closing, so if you've finished, I'll take your glass," she said quietly.

"Tully, I need to explain about the other day. I know you're upset and I don't blame you. I acted like a jerk. It's taken me this long to work up the nerve to apologize to you," he admitted and shook his head mournfully.

"Nothing to apologize for. I've forgotten all about it. Now can I have your glass?" She brushed his apology off without missing a beat and proudly congratulated herself for the good job. It sounded pretty believable.

"Tully—" He tried to speak but she firmly cut him off.

"Your glass, please"

With a frustrated sigh he slid over his glass and stood up. "I'll be waiting for you when you get home. We'll talk then." Judging by the stubborn tilt of his chin, she had little doubt he intended to follow through with his promise.

There were nights when it seemed to take forever to get the last of the patrons out and the clean-up finished, but tonight was not one of those nights. No matter how hard she tried to delay the inevitable, she could no longer put off going home.

She didn't have to wait that long to face him as it turned out. As she drew closer to her car, Jake was there leaning against the hood, arms across his chest, ankles crossed, waiting for her.

She slowed her steps and felt the charged atmosphere even before she came to a stop before him. "What are you doing here?"

"I don't trust that old bomb of yours and I didn't like the way a few of the younger guys in there tonight were looking at you. Figured I'd wait around in case there was any trouble." His tone was firm, and his eyes defiant, as he waited for her response.

"You're planning on being my chaperone from now on?" she asked, keeping her voice as light as she could manage even though inside she was fuming over his patronizing attitude.

"I'm just looking out for you." He shrugged.

"It's not necessary. I've been looking after myself for a long time now, Jake." She stepped around him and unlocked the driver's side door but before she could slide in behind the wheel, he caught her arm and stepped in closer.

"It's okay to depend on other people sometimes, Tully," he told her, his voice dropping to a low growl that made her stomach quiver, but to her horror, she felt tears begin to well in her eyes and angrily reefed her arm from his grasp.

"I learned the hard way not to depend on anyone else. It's the only way to avoid disappointment. Besides, you made yourself crystal clear the other day that you have absolutely no interest in me whatsoever, so just leave me alone." Her voice quivered and she dropped her gaze so he wouldn't see the telltale signs that it had hurt her a great deal.

"I didn't handle that well, I know that, and you have every right to think I'm a jerk, but I need to explain why."

"I don't want to talk about it, Jake. Let's just forget it."

"It wasn't you. You didn't do anything wrong. It was me." His own voice sounded less than steady as he searched her eyes for understanding. "My scars are reminders. Every day they remind me of how it happened. You were the first person other than the hospital staff who's seen them. I guess I just wasn't as ready as I thought I was. It was me, Tully. Not you."

She stared at him in disbelief. "You were *embarrassed* about your scars?" Her eyes softened. "I didn't realize. I'm sorry, it just didn't occur to me that a guy would..." Her sentence faded away as she searched for words.

"Have body image issues?" He finished for her dryly.

Tully cringed and nodded in agreement.

"Look, I've never been a SNAG or one of those new age metrosexuals," he said with a shudder that brought a smile to her lips. "It's not so much how it looks as how people react to how it looks, that bothers me." He dropped his eyes to the ground and shuffled his feet in the gravel aimlessly.

"Men died that day, people I knew. Friends." He paused, while he composed himself. "It's still a big deal and I need to work through a few of the things that happened over there. Until I come to terms with it all, I can't expect anyone else to."

There was a long silence as his words settled in the humid air between them.

"I just wanted you to understand it wasn't you, that's all." His voice was barely a whisper.

Tully bit her lip. She almost preferred to be angry at him. At least that made her feel in control of something. Anger she understood, anger could drive a person, give them the strength to overcome obstacles in their path, push them when they were at the end of their limits. However, what she felt at the moment was foreign to her. It wasn't pity—far from it. She admired Jake and the strength he'd summoned in order to survive the pain and torment of his injuries. What she felt was almost protective. The thought seemed ludicrous. The man before her looked like the last person in need of protection, from anything. Maybe she'd been working too hard and needed a break before she really started losing it! "Let's just forget it happened. I don't usually...I don't know what I was thinking." She finished and felt the heat rise in her face.

"Probably the same thing I was," he murmured and his gaze dropped to her lips. His voice took on a smoky, seductive tone that made her breath catch. "I never said I regretted anything that happened. The only regret I've had all week was that I was stupid enough to walk away." He slid his hands down her arms until he held her wrists. With gentle pressure he pulled her close enough to feel his breath, warm against her face.

Somewhere, on some level, Tully knew this was not a good idea, but it was almost impossible to resist the magnetic-like draw he sparked in her. Her breath caught in her throat and her eyes fluttered closed as she waited for the warmth of his mouth to press against her own.

The blast of a car horn ripped through the magic fog that had descended upon them and she pulled away, alarmed. The car, full of alcohol-brazen teenagers, disappeared in a blur of red taillights, leaving them to blink at each other in the awkward moments that followed.

"I need to get home." Tully ducked beneath his arm to slide into the driver's side of the car. She tugged at the door and reluctantly he stepped away to allow it to close.

"I'll follow you home to make sure the car starts," he sighed, his tone ironical.

Impatient to leave, she nodded and turned the key, fearful her car would choose this precise moment in which to become temperamental. With only the slightest puff of smoke the engine turned over and she breathed a sigh of relief as she pulled out of her park and headed home.

Tully was already at her front door by the time Jake pulled into the driveway. She waved what she hoped was a cheery good night and closed the door behind her.

The next morning, Tully lay in her bed rubbing her eyes as she tried to remember the dream she'd just had. She closed her eyes in dismay as her pulse raced rapidly. The things she'd dreamt were not things that *"just"* neighbors should be doing. With a frustrated sigh she headed for the shower and did her best to wash away the telltale flush from her skin. The visions in her head would be harder to erase.

Downstairs in the kitchen, still lost in lingering memories of the previous night's reverie, she had been staring into space through the kitchen window when Jake walked past on his way to her back door.

Startled, she lost her grip on the sudsy glass she'd been washing and it shattered into the sink, followed by a muttered curse. Quickly she wrapped a tea towel around her hand before crossing to the back door where Jake was waiting impatiently—eager to inspect the damage. "Sorry, I didn't mean to scare you. Show me your hand," he ordered, taking her wrist and leading her back toward the kitchen sink.

"It's not that bad." Tully protested to no avail as Jake unwrapped the tea towel and placed her hand under the tap. A few stray slivers of glass had lodged themselves in her hand.

"First aid kit?" His tone warned he was not about to listen to her arguments.

She told him where the kit was kept and, seated on a kitchen stool, watched as he cleaned and dressed her small wounds with confidence.

"There you go, good as new," he announced, holding her hand in his larger one and smiling down into her upturned face.

"Thank you, Doctor Holden, I'm sure I would have surely bled to death had you not happened along." She softened her sarcasm with a smile and removed her hand from his.

"You're welcome." His dry tone followed her from the kitchen as she took the bloodstained tea towels to the laundry.

"Coffee?" At his affable agreement, she turned to open the cupboard and collected two cups. Two arms appeared from behind her and took the cups from her hands to place them gently on the counter.

Tully could feel the heat radiating from his big body as he stood behind her, and fought to keep from turning to face him. She could almost feel the brush of skin, even through their clothing. "Sugar and milk?" Her voice trembled.

"Neither," he finally told her, stepping back and breaking the spell.

"Was there a reason you had to scare the living daylights out of me, or was it just a spur-of-the-moment decision?" she asked, keeping her face averted.

"I was knocking on your front door and didn't get a response, so I came around the back." He shrugged and nodded his thanks as she passed his cup across the kitchen counter toward him.

She squirmed as she recalled the erotic dream she'd been more than a little distracted by since waking and hoped he couldn't read her mind.

"I need a favor," he said without preamble.

She looked up when she caught the discomfort in his tone and felt a flicker of curiosity tweak inside her. What favor could the capable Jake Holden possibly need from her?

"What kind of favor?" She was unsettled by the way he fidgeted with the handle of his coffee cup.

"The only kind, of course, the one where I'm desperate or I wouldn't be asking you to help me out." His sigh sounded like that of a condemned man.

"I've been invited to a BBQ and I need you to come with me. I swear I can't make it through alone. If I have to fake an opinion one more time on the wrongs of pacifier usage or cloth versus disposable diapers, I'll jump off a cliff."

Tully chuckled, partly from relief but amused to witness the unflappable Jake Holden unravelling over a BBQ.

"It's not funny. I'm serious, I would do anything for any of those guys, but after the disaster at my place, I draw the line at doing the family thing solo."

"Then why did you agree to go? Just tell them you can't make it." She shrugged, took a sip of coffee and watched him over the top of her cup.

"Can't." He shook his head regretfully. "They used the mate card."

"The mate card?"

"Guilt trip," he explained, then mimicked in demonstration, *"Come on, mate, you gotta come."*

"I already told you I'm no better with my friends when it comes to family stuff," she reminded him.

"All I know is, two of us are a bigger target than just me on my own." He sat back and looked at her pleadingly. "Come on, Chambers, I'd do it for you."

"Yeah, right!" She chuckled, then set her cup down to eye him thoughtfully. "I'll go on one condition."

He sat up straighter. "Name it."

"You stop interrogating me."

He eyed her a few moments before giving a slow nod. "Deal."

The remainder of his coffee went in one gulp. Then he stood abruptly.

From across the counter, Tully lifted startled eyes and found they rested on his denim-covered groin. The material there, bunched from being seated, shifted and settled comfortably around a large bulge.

"We leave at midday."

His voice cut through the fog of lust which had descended upon her and she closed her eyes in mortification. When she opened them, he was gone. She doubted he'd even looked back.

She had the sneaking suspicion she'd just been had. *"Midday?"* She glanced up at the clock on the wall. It was already 11:00 a.m. Nothing like short notice, she thought irritably.

Why had she agreed to something she would normally have given a flat no to in any other circumstances? There was no time to contemplate. It was too late, and she'd already agreed to go.

At midday she walked out the front door and saw Jake leaning against his four-wheel drive, arms crossed and face tilted up to the sunshine. She paused to watch him, but as though he sensed her, he opened his eyes, and her heart skipped a beat.

"You look good in a dress, Chambers. You should show off those legs more often." He winked and allowed himself the rare opportunity to appreciate the tantalizing glimpse of cleavage the low neckline of her dress gave him.

She had debated over wearing the cheery red sundress and flat sandals. It was something she had bought but never had the chance to wear before today.

Thrown off guard by his compliment, Tully slid into the passenger seat and sat quietly as they headed through the laid-back, Saturday afternoon streets. The address was on the north side of Townsville and took some time to travel through the spread-out city.

The house was in a modern estate where the army had leased a great deal of homes to house its families. The streets were wide, full of children playing and people mowing lawns. This would be a great place to bring up a family. The thought made Tully fidget in her seat. Where on earth did that come from?

She rarely ever thought about a family of her own. A quick glance at Jake confirmed he looked nothing like a family man either. His knuckles clenched the wheel tightly and he seemed genuinely uncomfortable as he headed for what should be a pleasant BBQ with friends.

The house was white brick with a huge brown fence surrounding the front yard. Jake held open the gate for her to walk through and she waited as he closed it before they walked toward the noise out the back.

Jake had brought along a plastic bag with chips, dips, and paper plates. As they walked into the party, he handed the bag over to a small woman with a baby on one hip and a wine glass in the opposite hand.

"Tully, this is Jade, Matt's wife," he introduced briefly.

Tully nodded and smiled. The other couples seated around the table all looked up curiously as introductions were exchanged and Tully attempted to peg names to faces.

There were kids everywhere. They ran around the table, played on the swing set, jumped on the trampoline, and hung off adults everywhere she looked. Quickly glancing at Jake, she saw him nod his head in sympathy. No wonder he was intimidated. The noise and chaos was unnerving to say the least.

Jake seated her and disappeared to get drinks. When he came back he sat beside her and started talking with the man closest to him. It was clear all the men were close. They had served in the army for a long time together and were bonded by their experiences.

The women, too, seemed at ease and appeared to be a close-knit group. While not excluding her, it was difficult to do more than listen and nod politely since she had little in common with any of them. She did, however, feel a warm companionship she had not experienced in far too long.

Throughout the afternoon, Jake rarely left her side and she had to admit it was nice. At one stage, he dropped his arm across the back of her chair, as he talked to one of the men, and his arm lightly brushed her back. She felt a small quiver of delight flood through her. It was a simple gesture and probably made for no other reason than it was comfortable, but it stuck in her mind and warmed her for the remainder of the afternoon.

It was after seven when they got home and she was surprised to realize she had enjoyed herself. The women had invited her to come back whenever she felt like a visit, but with only Sundays off, it was unlikely she would be able to ever accept. Still, it was a nice offer, she'd thought.

"Thank you for coming today." Jake shuffled his feet on the path outside her apartment. A gentle breeze stirred, and she felt it caress her bare shoulders as the hem of her skirt floated around her legs.

"That's okay. It wasn't *that* bad."

He caught her eye and a grin spread across his face. "Tell me you're not thankful to the guy who invented the condom right now?"

Tully shook her head but shared his smile. It was alarming that only four couples had produced that many offspring.

"You want to go get something to eat?" he asked when neither of them made a move to go inside.

She shook her head and groaned, "I don't think I'll be able to eat for a week."

"You're really going to make me work for this, aren't you, Tully?"

Tully's gaze flew to his and an inner alarm began to ring. "Jake—I…"

"Yeah—I know. You can't get involved with anyone right now."

"I can't."

"Kinda not a word that's in my vocabulary."

Tully bit back a few words she could have added to his vocabulary, instead taking a step back, and giving him what she hoped was a discouraging glare. "Good night, Jake."

"It *could* have been, Tully. You have no idea what you're missin'," he told her with a grin.

Turning her back as she walked toward her front door, Tully tried to wipe the smile from her face, but couldn't. Jake Holden just didn't know when to give up.

* * * *

"So, Leonardo, have we made any progress on the little search we're doing?" The old man watched his son's eyes dart nervously toward the prison guards stationed around the room. He'd always been such a disappointment to him.

"We think we're getting closer, father. We should have a location soon, and then we can take care of that particular problem."

"I don't have to remind you how important this is to me, Leonardo, do I? This problem needs to be taken care of, soon."

It had to have been his mother, he thought bitterly. She'd always mollycoddled the boy. He should have been firmer with her about it.

"You can trust me, father. I will not let you down," the younger man vowed, and felt the emotion tightening his throat, squeezing the air from his lungs. He knew he had to make amends. It was he who had jeopardized the family, been responsible for the breach in which his father and many others had been arrested. It was through his weakness, his betrayal, his lust for a woman that the mighty Spiros family had begun to crumble.

Retribution was now the only thing on his mind; his pride as a man had been stripped away, leaving him raw and exposed. His reputation had been thrown to the ground and trampled beyond all recognition. White-hot hatred burnt inside, replacing the lustful, all consuming desire he'd had only a few months before.

Never would he lay open his heart as he had for this woman who had deceived him. He would seek his revenge, restore his family's pride and trust in him, and he would make his father proud once more.

He would make her pay for his disgrace.

* * * *

When Tully finished work the next Saturday evening, she discovered a note on her front door. Cautiously she pulled it loose from the tape and read by the light of her key ring flashlight.

You are cordially invited to a late supper at the residence of Mister Jake Holden, Esquire. Please note nonattendance will be met with severe punishment!

The cautious, sane part of her wanted to walk inside and ignore the invitation, but another side of her had begun to emerge, the free falling, bungee-jumping part that, hard as she tried to ignore it, had become more than a little curious.

She knocked on Jake's door and waited for him to answer with a stomach that bubbled and fizzed in nervous expectation.

The door opened and Jake stood there, dominating the doorway even as he wore a cautious grin. "Glad you could make it."

"I wanted to see how an *esquire* lives."

"Here I was thinking you were intimidated by the threat of severe punishment," he murmured, allowing her to precede him into the house.

His unit appeared much the same as her own, although his carpet was a soft grey with charcoal and off-white tones on the walls, not the blues and creams in her place. He also had air-conditioning throughout his unit and she sighed with barely concealed jealousy.

Two soft sofas in dark grey suede beckoned invitingly. While he went to bring out the food, she took her time to explore. She let her gaze wander along the book titles and skim across the faces and places of pictures in chunky silver frames.

The pictures, mostly of Jake and others in army fatigues, showed them posing with guns and grins in some, while in others he seemed deadly serious and not nearly so approachable.

His reading tastes ranged from crime thrillers to biographies and war stories. When she'd finished inspecting the shelves she wandered out to his kitchen and waited as he served two plates of food.

"Very domesticated, Holden," she complimented.

"Just one of my talents," he agreed with a sly grin.

Tully rolled her eyes and continued surveying the room. All his appliances were new, gleaming stainless steel and state of the art. He followed her gaze and gave the fridge a proud pat. "You like my latest additions?"

"You certainly have good taste...and a healthy budget," she added dryly.

He shrugged offhandedly. "I've lived in army barracks most of my life. When I got out I decided to splash out on some decent stuff."

He nodded at the dining table, a gorgeous stainless steel with frosted-glass top design, set with bamboo place mats and a single candle in the center.

"This is impressive."

"I noticed when you get home from your shift at the bar you always make something to eat." When she raised an eyebrow in suspicion, he hastily explained, "The walls...I hear you banging around in there...Anyway, just thought I'd spare myself tonight and cook something for you instead."

Shaking her head at his exaggerated protest of her nocturnal habits, she picked up a fork and stabbed a tender piece of chicken from her plate. "Wow, you really can cook."

"You don't have to sound quite so surprised," he complained, but appeared satisfied that she'd approved.

He poured two glasses of an expensive wine and she savored the taste on her tongue.

Tully began to unwind as the wine surged merrily through her veins and the food filled her stomach. "Let's move into the living room. You look like you're about to fall asleep at the table."

"I should go home."

"Just once, Chambers—can you live dangerously and do what feels right for a change?"

"*Feeling* right and *knowing* right are two very different things, Jake."

"When was the last time you did something just 'cause it *felt* good?"

"This morning," she said, surprising him with her automatic response.

"Really? What did you do?" he asked, his voice dropping into a suggestive low tone as his man-mind raced with all kinds of kinky fantasies a woman might do to feel good alone in the morning.

"I made myself coffee."

"Yep. See. No idea how to live," he told her, leading the way into the living room. Indicating she should take a seat, Tully sent him an exasperated glance. His only reply was to cock one eyebrow in a silent challenge, and damned if it didn't grate on her nerves to back down. "Fine. I'll stay for coffee...and that's all!" she called as he disappeared back into the kitchen before she could change her mind.

Tipping her head back to rest on the back of the soft lounge chair, Tully felt the wine seeping into her bloodstream—sending a relaxing buzz throughout her body.

Coming back into the room with the coffee, Jake cleared his throat softly and Tully opened her eyes and sat up straighter, startled as she realized she must have almost dozed off. *You must be really losing your edge, Chambers,* she thought to herself.

Jake took a seat beside her on the couch—his thigh pressing along the length of her own felt warm and solid. Tully quickly leaned forward to take her cup from the coffee table in front of them, in order to distract herself from the sudden lewd thoughts running through her head.

"Tell me about them," Tully said, nodding her head toward the photos of his army mates on the wall to distract him from making any sudden moves on her, but as he spoke, she found herself smiling at the stories he told.

"Do you keep in touch with them now you're out of the army?"

"Yeah—most of them."

At his hollow expression, she realized too late that some of the men on the wall were probably those killed in the incident that almost claimed his own life and kicked herself for not being a little more sensitive.

Placing a hand over the top of his that rested on his thigh beside her, Tully gave it a gentle squeeze, and held the gaze he turned from the wall across the room to meet her own. "There's no reason why some make it and some don't. It's just the way it is."

"Doesn't make it any easier to live with though, Tully," he said quietly and the pain in his voice pulled at her heart. He was right—it certainly didn't make it any easier.

Moved by a shared heartache, Tully found herself leaning toward him, wanting to forget that emptiness and guilt—needing to find a release for the nightmares and endless sorrow of losing someone you loved like a brother.

It was not a gentle kiss—Jake took what she offered without a second's hesitation, and Tully found that his need ignited her own. For a long time they seemed to devour each other—both fighting their own demons until the sting of remembering dulled, and the throb of desire took over.

A shiver of delight raced through her body as his lips moved like a butterfly's caress against her neck and she tipped her face back to allow him further access. Deep inside her a warm glow began to spread through parts of her she'd long denied having anyone pay attention to. His touch grew bolder, his kisses harder along the exposed length of her neck and she shivered as he ran his tongue slowly, deliciously along her skin. Tasting her, savoring her like some long-denied indulgence.

Catching her breath, she pulled back slightly. His gaze, hot and simmering, sent a shot of liquid desire that went straight to her loins.

He bent his head and caught her lips, dragging a response from someplace deep inside her she'd almost forgotten existed.

His probing tongue teased and caressed her own, tangling, enticing, and daring her to take the lead. Spurred on by his silent challenge, she deepened the kiss, nipping and biting his sensitive lower lip, until a deep groan of approval escaped his chest and vibrated through her own.

Something primeval and urgent broke free inside her, and a need to be touched and to touch in return took control. The scent of desire radiating between them drove her to deepen the kiss. She suckled gently on the fullness of his lower lip, and felt the immediate swell of his groin press urgently against her belly as his hands slid around her hips and moved lower to cup her backside, pulling her firmly against him.

With a muffled curse against her mouth, he lifted her off the ground to hug his lean hips. Her legs automatically circled his hips snugly.

"Living room or bedroom?" he asked against her mouth.

"How long will it take you to get us upstairs?" she asked, her voice sounding breathless.

He smiled beneath her mouth as she continued to drag her own lips against his, reluctant to interrupt the drug-like addiction of his kisses. "That depends...what's the magic word?" he teased, pulling his head away from her tempting lips to taunt her.

"Now?"

His slow, sexy grin spread across his face and he gave a nod as he moved toward the staircase. "Close enough." Without breaking the hold on her lips, he climbed the stairs and maneuvered them into his bedroom.

With deliberate slowness he allowed her to slide down the length of his body until her feet touched the ground. His eyes glittered with sensual satisfaction at the delicious torture the friction evoked between them.

"You sure about this?"

"Why are you still talking?" Tully growled impatiently.

With gentle hands, he lifted her arms and removed her shirt. Standing before him in a white silk bra, the gentle swell of her breast strained against the fabric as he feasted his hungry gaze upon them. She held her breath as he lightly traced his fingertips around the hardened centers. Then, with a flick of his fingers, he unclasped the front fastening, watching as her breasts tumbled free and fell into his waiting hands.

She gasped as the rush of cool air against her skin was immediately followed by the warmth of his hands. Mesmerized, she looked down at his dark, roughened hands against the white firm flesh of her breasts and a shiver of longing rippled through her body.

"You're so beautiful."

Beautiful? Her?

She watched in amazement as his head lowered and his mouth closed upon one tight bud. A gasp of delight escaped and he continued his onslaught. She stood, gripping his shoulders tightly, her head thrown back in rapturous abandon as her body moved against him in a timeless rhythm of desire.

Beautiful. In this moment she'd never felt more beautiful...or alive.

Gently he lowered her onto his bed until she felt the caress of cool silk beneath her heated skin. Discarding the remainder of their clothing, he rolled her beneath him and she sizzled as the weight of his body and heat of his skin scorched her from inside.

He held her gaze steadily and she knew he was waiting, offering, even at this late stage, a chance for her to put a stop to it.

"Has it been that long you've forgotten what to do, soldier boy?"

She watched him reach over her to the bedside table and withdraw a box of condoms. It took a few minutes to dig out a small parcel and Tully arched an eyebrow.

"Brand new box. Someone was feeling optimistic." She took the packet from his fingers, ripping it open and rolling the condom over him slowly as he watched quietly, with patient amusement.

"That smart mouth of yours is going to land you in a world of trouble someday, Chambers," he drawled lazily, his eyes darkening as she moved beneath him deviously.

"I'm counting on it."

Nudging her thigh against his hardness with a sultry smile, she drew an appreciative chuckle from his chest, which soon became a long, rugged groan as he pushed against the softness of her welcoming warmth.

He smiled as a shudder of delight rippled through her quivering body beneath him.

Slowly he moved within her, his arms braced beside her, muscles bunching with each stroke. His body glistened with sweat, making him sleek and slippery in the shimmering pale moonlight as it spilt across the room from the open window. A gentle breeze rippled the curtains, its touch like a second lover's caress as it whispered across their damp bodies.

The air became heavy with the scent of their sex, a sweet,

musky fragrance that assaulted her senses. Next to her ear she heard Jake breathe, a guttural, panting sound that echoed in her own panting and drove her to the edge of reason.

His thrusts pushed deep inside, filling her, stretching her. Tully dug her fingers into his shoulders, urging him onwards as her muscles contracted and pulled him even more deeply inside her. The tempo increased, his body slammed into hers. Tully arched her back beneath him, her mouth whispering a soundless moan as her internal inferno swelled and throbbed, hot and needy.

He must have sensed she was nearing the peak, and confirmed it when he all but groaned near her ear, "Just let it go, come with me, Tully..."

Opening her eyes, she stared up into his hooded, heavy gaze, his face taut and straining as he held back his own climax until she could follow him over the edge. She clenched around him tightly and he jerked in response, his thrusts escalating wildly. She felt herself contract and spasm around him as her release triggered his own. He stiffened, releasing a warm pool of desire deep inside her before collapsing against her.

Rolling them so they lay side by side, he held her as their breathing slowed and the gentle night breeze cooled their sweating bodies.

Moments later Jake rolled away briefly, and she heard him fumbling in the dark before he turned back, drawing her close once more. Her head rested on his chest and the weight of his arm across her hip felt comforting, but long after his breathing had evened out and his heartbeat steadied beneath her ear, Tully remained awake...lost in her thoughts and the uncomfortable feeling that she'd just stepped over a very fragile line.

Chapter Five

"Where are you going?" Jake could see his lazy question had startled Tully as she tried to gather her clothing quietly in the early morning light.

"To work. I'm sure you've heard of it." She zipped up her jeans and tucked in her shirt.

So that's how she wanted to play it. He caught her hand in his and held it firmly. "Call in sick. Stay here and play with me."

Tully chuckled, and he was surprised by the release of fear he hadn't realized he'd been masking. "Some of us have work ethics, and not all of us can sit around watching Doctor Phil at our leisure."

She disentangled her fingers from his and flashed him a rare smile that softened the blow, and with a promise to see him after work, left without a backward glance. Jake wasn't so sure he liked that she could leave him so easily, but rather than dwell on that unexpected thought, he chose to look forward to the fact that she said she'd be back.

He listened to his front door closing behind her and a satisfied smile spread across his face as he laced his hands behind his head and thought back over the night's events. It had been even better than he'd dared to imagine, and boy, had he been imagining it! The woman had been driving him insane ever since they'd met. Images of smooth skin and long legs, her deep-throated groans and happy sighs of pleasure bombarded him, forcing him out of bed and into a cold shower. It was going to be a very long day as he waited for her to finish work.

As he made his way downstairs, barefoot and whistling, he continued to ride his morning afterglow, and felt content with his lot. He headed toward the living room and picked up the remote to flick on his oversized, macho TV screen. He was man enough to admit when it came to his toys, bigger was definitely better and his splurge on this giant had had him grinning like a kid at Christmas the day it was delivered.

While he fried up bacon and eggs, he listened to the morning news but soon turned off the pan to head back into the living room as a segment caught his attention.

"Police are today suffering a huge setback in the ongoing mob boss trial of Aeneas Spiros. Early this morning the body of a key witness was discovered in bushland south of the city. Foul play has not been ruled out due to the impending involvement of the deceased man in the infamous Spiros family indictment case due to commence in the next few weeks. Investigations are continuing into the death and we will bring you any further developments as they come to hand.

"Meanwhile, the chief commissioner of Victoria Police has said while this is a major blow to the prosecution's defense, the Spiros family's accountant was not the only witness the prosecution had. He went on to say that society would not be cowed by certain factions within the business community who continue to use violence to secure their position. He stopped short of condemning the Spiros family for the murder of the witness, but has said nobody is above the law."

Jake stood in front of his big TV, legs wide, arms folded, as he tried to figure out what bugged him about this story. With a thoughtful frown he wandered back out to the kitchen to finish cooking breakfast, but his mind was so busy digesting the bits and pieces of information he'd been gathering in his quest to uncover his sexy next-door neighbor's secrets he almost burnt the bacon.

* * * *

Tully's day was going from bad to worse. She was decidedly on edge. What was she thinking? She wasn't supposed to be involved with anyone while she was here. What had happened to keeping a low profile? Had she learned nothing from the past? Involving anyone in her life was subjecting them to the possibility of danger.

Clearing a table after her first customer of the day, Tully reached for the discarded newspaper and froze as her gaze fell upon the photo on the front page. In the center, a large photo of what looked like a crime scene in bushland caught her attention, but it was the smaller photo in the top corner that froze her breath in her lungs. Quickly she skimmed the article, her unease growing with each word as she tried to absorb what it all meant.

She was the only one left.

Sinking onto a chair, Tully lifted her gaze from the paper and stared out at the busy strand, seeing through the tourists enjoying a pleasant stroll along the water's edge. While outwardly she tried to stay calm, inside, her mind was in overdrive. They'd killed the accountant. She couldn't believe it. The key witness in the whole damn trial! A bitter curse escaped and Tully quickly glanced around, relieved to see the café was empty, and forced herself to calm down.

The urge to flee hovered anxiously around her and it took a great deal of concentration to force it back. She needed to think—not react. They wanted her to run—it was the only way they'd be able to flush her out in the open. She was safe here. She just needed to hold it together for a little longer without making any mistakes. *Just keep your head down and you'll be fine,* she lectured herself firmly. *You've made it this far.*

As the day wore on, her jumpy nerves didn't settle. If anything, they got worse.

She headed over to a customer who had just sat down and prepared to take his order. Meeting his eyes, she felt something inside her shift. For the briefest of moments she felt a tingle of unease run down her spine.

Tully blinked and the feeling went away. She didn't know this man, but for an instant something about him reminded her of someone she'd known before. A trickle of sweat made its way down her back and Tully blinked again to get rid of the tiny black dots that floated before her eyes. When it happened a second time later that afternoon, she decided it was her mind playing tricks on her.

It wasn't. A loud rushing roared in her ears as she stared at the man seated at the table. She watched his mouth move but was unable to hear what he was saying.

I have a message for you, she heard in her mind as her legs began to tremble.

Tully felt the color leave her face and she began to sway. Something inside her cracked, and panic like she had never before experienced clawed and scratched its way to the surface.

"What did you say?" she demanded, although her voice came out barely a whisper.

He looked at her strangely, as though he were expecting her to pass out at any moment. "I just asked for a coffee and a muffin," he said, somewhat apprehensively. "Are you all right?"

Tully shook her head as though in a trance. What was happening to her? Now she was hearing things as well. She took a break out the back, to regain her fast-retreating senses, and tried not to become alarmed as she realized her heart was still racing. She was having some kind of anxiety attack. She'd seen them many times before, in other people, but she'd never imagined experiencing one herself. The door opened and she wiped at her face discreetly.

"Tully, is everything all right? You don't seem your usual self." The gentle words came from the birdlike woman who ran the café along with her Santa Claus look-alike husband. Mrs. Winters wore her long dark hair in a tight bun on top of her head and, even though she was tiny, there was no mistaking who ran the show.

"I'm really sorry I haven't been able to focus today," Tully apologized wearily.

"You should have called in sick and taken the day off. Honestly, Tully, sometimes I wonder if you realize you are still human."

Tully stared at the small woman before her in confusion. "Excuse me?" she asked uncertainly.

The older woman gave a click of her tongue in exasperation. "It's obvious that something terribly traumatic has happened to you and you're still recovering from it. I knew the day you came in here looking for a job you were special. That's why I gave you the job on the spot—but you need to take care of yourself." Her voice dropped to a gentleness that tugged at Tully's heart. "Whatever it is you're running from will eventually catch up with you if you don't stop and confront it soon," the older woman warned before smiling softly. "Go home, Tully, and take some time off. We'll still be here when you're ready to come back to us." She patted Tully's arm softly and turned away.

Tully stood watching the older woman's back in a daze. Had she just been fired? What exactly had just happened here? This was not good. Nothing had been going right since she had met Jake Holden. Damn that man!

She knew what needed to be done.

She ran herself harder than usual on the way home, taking a longer route and pushing her body to go faster. She would try and run the anxiety out of her system, if all else failed. She didn't have room in her life at the moment for men and mixed emotions. This was a big part of why she'd given men in general a wide berth. For the next few weeks it was vital she keep a clear head—and she'd already established Jake Holden was not conducive to keeping her faculties straight by any stretch of the imagination.

* * * *

When Jake knocked on her door later that evening, he seemed

somewhat subdued.

"Tell me about Spiros," he said without preamble, his face taut and his eyes more serious than she'd ever seen them before.

For the second time that day, Tully felt the color drain from her face. She turned away but he didn't give her time to compose herself. Instead he turned her to look at him. "You were acting weird the other day when you saw the story in the paper about this Spiros guy. Are you in some kind of trouble?"

His gaze flickered, almost involuntarily, toward the drawer where her gun rested. Tully closed her eyes, not sure if she wanted to laugh or cry. Trust her to find the one man on the planet who observed things no one else would have even thought twice about.

"I want you to leave, Jake." When he opened his mouth to protest she added, "Now."

Jake left, but was not deterred. He waited for the late news and knew he was on to something. The same newsreel that had aired that morning was featured again, but there was an added segment that contained older footage immediately after it.

The camera switched to footage of the day the arrest of Aeneas Spiros had taken place, a group of police and detectives swooping on the estate of the arrested billionaire.

As he watched the replay, he suddenly sat forward and paused the program. Searching the remote in his hand, he located the playback button and reran the footage. He would have missed it if it hadn't been for this marvel of new technology. Slowly clicking forward he found the picture he'd glimpsed and paused it once more. Sitting back in his seat he stared at the image before him on his huge plasma screen in all its fifty-inch glory.

On the screen was a harried, but identical twin of Tully, sliding into the front seat of an unmarked police car.

At least it looked like Tully, except the woman on the TV had shoulder length dark hair. Her eyes were hidden behind dark sunglasses and she wore tailored slacks and a jacket. Admittedly it was a very suave version of Tully, but it was her all right. With a soft whistle he collapsed back in the couch, dumbfounded.

"What the hell have you gotten yourself into, Chambers?"

Chapter Six

"What do you want, Jake?" Tully sighed, her forehead resting against the doorjamb wearily as she opened the door to his insistent pounding later that night.

Wordlessly he handed her the photo he'd taken from his computer earlier.

"Where did you get this?" she breathed fearfully, her face going pale as she stared at an image of her in the front seat of a police car.

"Tell me what's going on, Tully," he said softly, tipping her face up to meet his eyes. "You don't have to handle this alone."

Jake saw her slender shoulders shake and his heart tore clean in half. Reaching out, he pulled her stiff body toward him and held her. Even as she struggled, he just held her until she stopped, and listened to the small sobs as they escaped against his wide chest and warm tears soaked his shirt. He wasn't sure how long they stood there, but eventually her tears subsided and after a few minutes she wiped her face and straightened her shoulders. She stepped out of his embrace and refused to meet his eyes.

"How are you involved, Tully?"

With a shattered sigh, she rubbed her face briskly, and led him into the apartment. She was too tired to fight anymore. "I'm a witness in the Spiros case."

"What the hell are you doing here? Why don't you have any protection?" he demanded with an incredulous expression. "We need to go to the police, get you some security."

"Jake, I *am* the police," she said quietly. "I'm a detective with the Victorian police force."

"A detective?" His hands clenched tightly on the back of the kitchen chair he leaned on. He stared at her, a mixture of disbelief and betrayal stamped across his face. "Can't say I saw that one coming, but I guess it explains a lot."

"It's no big deal. I've been living like this for the last five months. It's only a few more weeks until the trial. Once I give my testimony, it will be all over."

"Let me get this straight. You're a detective and you've been in hiding from a crazed mob boss who's got a grudge against you because you sent him to prison?"

"Well, that and the fact I'm about to testify against him," she added with a twist of her lips.

Jake gave a small grunt in response.

"His son, Leo Spiros, killed my partner. When an opportunity to work undercover came up, I took it. We blew the case wide open. They have lots of contacts including, possibly, some in the police force itself. Once my cover was blown I was suddenly at the top of the family's hit list. Apparently, I still am. I effectively have to disappear until the court case in a few weeks' time." She met his eyes. "Until then, everything is on hold, my job, my identity, my entire life." Her tone held a bitterness she couldn't hide. "My boss doesn't even know where I am or how to contact me. I have contact only by pre-paid cell phone with the task force leader."

Jake sat quietly, trying to digest her story.

"I was advised to get out of town. These people have their fingers in an awful lot of pies. We just don't have enough manpower to guard against an enemy we can't see coming." She moved away, needing to pace in order to gather her thoughts.

Jake couldn't imagine being so totally alone. In the army, he'd always had someone to watch his back. His mates were always there for him. It was the way he was trained, the way he had lived. From what he could see, Tully had no one. He studied her standing across from him, arms wrapped protectively around her body, and made a correction. She had him, and he was sure as hell not going to stand by and let her handle this alone.

"Well, you won't have to do this on your own anymore."

"Just because we slept together..." She paused, pulling the chair out across the table from him. "...Doesn't mean I'm your responsibility. I won't risk your life for something that had nothing to do with you."

"It's not your decision to make," he told her grimly. "You might be able to switch your emotions on and off, but you can't do the same to someone else's. I spent my entire adult life in a job where I had to follow orders, but don't make the mistake of thinking for one second I'll quietly bow out of your life just because you think it's for my own good. I get a say in this too."

"It's all irrelevant now anyway. I've decided to go back and end this one way or the other," she told him briskly and stood. When she brushed past him he grabbed her hand, halting her escape.

"You can't go back now. You won't last five minutes once they know you're back in town, not after they killed that last witness. I won't let anything happen to you," he said softly.

Tully's eyes misted. "Jake, I need you to keep your distance. I don't want you involved in this."

"How do you think you're going to handle this alone?" Jake clenched his jaw. How could one woman be this frustrating?

She pulled her hand out of his grasp. "I'm safe enough as long as they don't know where I am."

"I hate to bust ya bubble, Detective, but your face was just plastered across national TV. You don't think that's going to tip off a few people?"

"I doubt anyone who knows me here would recognize me from that old footage," she dismissed with a small shake of her head.

"I recognized you," he pointed out dryly.

"You're more observant than most people," she shot back, then stepped away. "I need to think this through and I can't do that right now."

"You need to get some sleep," he told her firmly.

Tully turned furious eyes upon him. "I *need* to make up my own damn mind, not have you bulldoze your way into my life and take over."

"Well, excuse me for giving a damn." His voice was rough, with not the slightest hint of apology detectable.

"Jake, I have never needed a man to make my decisions and I'm not about to start now."

Jake saw the resolve in her tired eyes. He'd sensed from the very first minute she was more than capable of handling herself in most situations, but he also knew she meant something to him, and although the thought of a woman getting this far beneath his skin would have once sent him running for the hills, knowing it was Tully somehow made it all right. It also made him determined that nothing was going to happen to her.

"I'm not trying to run your life. I'm just trying to help you, Tully. Drop the tough cop act and just accept the offer for what it is. I'm not about to threaten your self-contained little system you have going here," he said, waving his hand toward the bare walls and empty rooms. "So relax."

He saw her weighing up his words—could almost hear her mind ticking over as she calculated the risk he posed to her precious independence. He could tell she wasn't convinced, and she was sure as hell not happy about it, but she also looked too tired to put up much of a fight over it anymore tonight.

He'd take whatever victory he could get right now, but didn't for a second think she considered this discussion was over.

She turned away from him silently, leaving him in the center of the room.

"I'm staying tonight. I'll be down here if you need anything." He called after her as he watched her walk upstairs without comment, and stifled a frustrated sigh before turning his thoughts ahead to what would need to be done.

* * * *

True to his word, Jake spent the night camped out in her living room but was up making coffee when Tully came downstairs the next morning. He glanced over at her briefly, giving her a nod of welcome and handing her a cup.

"You certainly know the way to a girl's heart, Holden," she murmured, and he hid a grin as he watched her inhale the coffee in rapturous delight.

"This girl, apparently," he murmured back, searching her face for any sign of last night's aftereffects. She seemed okay, if a little quiet. "You going in to work?" He raised an eyebrow.

"I was tactfully asked not to come back after I scared away a customer yesterday, so no, just the bar tonight. I need to keep busy, and the money comes in handy, considering I can't surface to collect my police paycheck," she added with a dryness that verged on brittle.

"Tully, you don't need to work if it's only a matter of money. I can take care of that," he told her without hesitation.

She turned away from him and he saw her shoulders tense and her head drop before she turned back and gave him a tight, "Thanks, but I prefer to work and pay my own way. I still have my shifts at the Bluey."

He watched without comment as she finished her coffee and placed the cup in the sink. A screen had come down between them. He wasn't sure why but he backed off and let the matter drop. He really was out of his depth with this woman.

He liked to take care of women. His mother had instilled a strong belief in him from a young age that men were *supposed* to take care of women. She'd been bitterly let down by his father in that department but it hadn't stopped her drumming it into her son. It was his experience, however, that women who *needed* to be taken care of became too needy and it had never worked out.

Tully, though, seemed to be on the other end of the scale.

Jake did know enough to realize he was outstaying his welcome now, and decided to give her some space. "I have a few things to take care of, so I'll see you later."

"Thanks for last night," she said softly.

He gave her a grin, and inside felt a little bit of his warrior's heart soften.

* * * *

The street was quiet with only the odd drunken patrons refusing to call it a night as they staggered through the empty city center. Tully always parked under a streetlight and was careful to check the area before unlocking her car. It wasn't the crime capital of Australia, but her years on the force had taught her to be vigilant about personal safety. Women alone at night would always be an easy target for some criminals no matter where they lived.

As she drove through the darkened streets, her tired muscles began to relax. The traffic lights ahead turned red and she slowed to a stop with her indicator clicking loudly in the silence. A glance in her mirror showed a dark four-wheel drive with shiny wheels turning onto the street and pulling up behind her. For a moment she thought it was Jake, but a quick squint at the number plate in her mirror showed that it wasn't him.

Jake.

She'd been thinking about him all day. Their night together had been more than she'd ever expected and it wasn't just the great sex—she couldn't remember the last time she'd allowed herself to feel something other than a basic need to blow off steam. Men had not been high on her list of priorities. They tended to complicate things and disrupt her well-ordered life and besides that, her choices were limited—she refused to date men she worked with and since she practically *lived* at work there were very few opportunities to meet any.

Then along came Jake Holden, throwing her self-discipline, not to mention self-preservation out the window.

What was happening to her? She was a seasoned detective—she always had a plan, an idea where she was headed, a solution for everything...until now. Here, she was in new territory, both physically and emotionally.

The lights changed and Tully pulled away, noticing the car behind her also turned. As she touched the accelerator, the four-wheel drive dropped back and Tully stayed a comfortable distance in front of the other vehicle.

The remainder of the lights were all green. With little traffic to hinder her it was a quick drive home at this hour of the morning. As she approached her street, Tully indicated and watched as the four-wheel drive behind her continued straight ahead.

Parking her car in the driveway, she stole a quick glance at Jake's unit and saw the place was in darkness.

Tully stepped out of her car and then muttered under her breath as she dropped her keys, fumbling in the dark as she re-trieved them from their resting place beneath the car. As she straightened, she glanced in the side mirror and paused. In the reflection was a dark four-wheel drive with shiny wheels parked outside in the street.

Shit.

A chill raced up her spine and she felt her heartbeat pick up no-ticeably. Careful to keep her movements calm, she walked around the front of the car and into the front door stoop of her unit. She opened her bag and removed a gun, *the other gun,* the one Jake didn't know about and tucked it into the back of her jeans. She always kept a weapon with her, concealed in her backpack or bag, within reach when she was out of the unit for occasions such as these.

Instead of going inside she ducked low and, keeping to the shadows behind the car in her driveway, snuck through the gar-den beds and made her way out into the street, circling behind the four-wheel drive. Crouching low in the shadows, Tully slowly reached back and removed the gun from the back of her jeans. She assessed the situation before her. There was only one person, the driver, and his focus was fixed on her front door.

Still crouching, she moved along the side of the car and in one quick movement opened the back door and jammed the gun to the temple of the driver who still wore his seat belt and was unable to move away in time.

"Why are you following me and who sent you?" Tully demand-ed, keeping her voice low and controlled. She felt his body tense, and saw his eyes widen in surprise in the rearview mirror.

"Hey, it's not what you think. Put the gun away." The man spoke quietly and calmly and in the back of her mind she regis-tered that he seemed quite professional.

"What am I supposed to think? You're sitting outside my house and you followed me from where I work, so I'll ask you again, who sent you?"

Tully held the driver's eyes in the mirror and put a little more pressure on his temple with her gun.

"I'm here because it was my shift. Jake asked a few of us to keep an eye on you. Apparently you've gotten yourself in a bit of trouble and he's worried enough to call in a lot of favors to keep you safe."

Tully's eyes narrowed in suspicion. "Jake? Jake Holden had you follow me?" she demanded, disbelief turning to fury.

"Put the gun down, and we'll call him out here so you can take it up with him. I'd really rather you had the gun against his head and not mine," the man in the mirror told her dryly.

Tully thought it over without moving the gun, before deciding to take the risk and let him go. "Call him outside," Tully said, following his slow movements warily with her eyes. The man in the driver's seat moved his thumb over the keypad and put the phone to his ear, watching her with just as much caution.

"It's me. You might wanna come outside for a minute and explain why I'm out here in my car with a gun at my head." He disconnected the call, his attention shifting to the door of the unit next to hers. Within seconds Jake came out the front door and Tully saw him take in the situation with a defeated shake of his head.

"Tully, it's okay. He's on our side," Jake said as he moved toward the car, his hands up in a nonthreatening way.

With a frustrated growl, she pushed open the door and slammed it shut behind her. "Our side, Jake? *Our* side?" she repeated, raising her voice and looking up into his impassive face. "There is no *our* side."

Feeling shaken, Tully took a deep breath before she could continue. "I put a gun to your friend's head, Jake. He scared the hell out of me. Why the hell have you got people following me?"

"Despite what you think, you can't do this alone and I'll be damned if I'm going to stand by and let something happen to you," he hissed, then made an effort to calm down. "I should have told you, and for that I apologize, but I knew you'd freak out if I did."

"Damn it, Jake." She threw her arms up in sheer frustration. "I can't talk to you right now!" She pushed past his big frame planted firmly in front of her and didn't look back, but heard Jake exchanging words with his friend. The sudden adrenaline rush she had just experienced had completely wiped her out and she felt teary and emotional, something she had no intention of showing Jake or his sidekick.

She headed straight for the shower. The hot water pounded against her back and immediately she felt her tense shoulders begin to relax. For as long as she could remember she had taken care of herself. She liked it that way, knew things were done right when she handled it. There was no chance of disappointment or being let down if she did things herself.

Hadn't living with her mother shown her that? She'd watched her mother move from one man to another, never happy when she was alone, always needing someone to take care of her, but somehow ending up with men who treated her like dirt. Each boyfriend a carbon copy of the one before, until finally she met the man who'd killed her—

Abruptly Tully shut down her train of thought. She was not her mother.

Wrapped in her silky robe, hair still damp from her shower, Tully sat down on her couch and opened her laptop. She stared at the screen as it went through its start-up routine and thought about the email she was going to write.

A firm knock tapped at the front door and Tully ignored it. At the second tap, she called out loudly, "Go away, Jake, I'm fine."

His only response was the sound of a key turning in the lock, followed by his large frame walking into the living room completely undaunted by the less-than-welcoming look on her face.

"I can't wait to hear how you're going to justify stealing my front door key. This should be really good," Tully said, still seated on the couch, arms folded across her chest.

"I didn't steal your key, Tully. Landlords are entitled to a spare key."

"You got it from my landlord?" She gaped at him in astonishment. Was he totally insane?

"I am your landlord," he told her, sitting down beside her on the couch and watching her with a smug grin.

She knew her mouth must have been gaping open, but he'd rendered her completely speechless with his little bombshell.

"I guess I forgot to mention that," he apologized without even attempting to sound the least bit sorry.

"I can see how it was so insignificant that it might slip your mind," she threw at him sarcastically.

"I should have slipped it into the conversation...when?"

"Oh, I don't know, how about, 'Hi, I'm Jake from next door and I also own your unit. Just thought I'd introduce myself'!"

He pursed his lips slightly, pretending to consider it. "Before or after you threw me over your shoulder?"

She closed her eyes, mortified. It was a wonder he hadn't had her evicted the next day.

Forcing calmness into her tone, she tried to reason with him. "Jake, you can't just storm in here and take over. This is not some kind of game. I thought your friend was someone Spiros sent. I could have *killed* him. Do you understand?"

Jake held her imploring eyes, his face a stoic mask. "I can assure you I don't think this is a game. I've researched this Spiros guy, read everything I can find on the Internet about the story, and I'm here to tell you, there's no way I'm going to risk that bastard finding you."

"I'm not a child! You have no right pushing your way into my life. Who the hell do you think you are?" Her chest heaved with indignation, and her eyes darkened in anger.

Taking her hand, he placed it across his chest and looked deep into her eyes. "I'll tell you who I'm *not*. I'm *not* the man who is going to let you push him away. So deal with it."

Chapter Seven

As she left the club, Tully waved good-bye to Terry the bouncer and crossed the street heading for the parking lot. A strange tingle ran across the nape of her neck and she felt her senses go into full alert. She'd been jumpy lately, fighting the constant urge to look over her shoulder ever since Jake and his buddies had effectively scared her witless last time they'd tried to shadow her. The fact that he'd never actually agreed to take off her unwanted body-guards suggested they were still lurking out there somewhere, this time with far more covert modus operandi in place.

Somehow, this feeling was different.

She slid her hand inside her handbag, and took comfort in the feel of the cold metal beneath her fingertips. She cast a careful look about her but could see nothing unusual, and yet she had the unshakable feeling something was wrong.

With keys in hand, she quickly unlocked the driver's side and opened her door. She started the car, nerves on edge, and battled to keep her attention on the road. As she darted glances into her rearview mirror she expected at any moment to see a sinister car tailing her.

When she arrived home she gave herself a mental shake. If she didn't pull herself together she would turn into a basket case by the time the trial came around. She slid the front door key into the lock just as she heard a slight scuffle behind her and turned in alarm.

It happened so fast she barely had time to register the fact that someone had grabbed her.

A cold voice whispered into her ear to open the door and with her arm twisted behind her back, she had little option but to do as she was told. He pushed her forward into the dark. Through the cloud of pain she could make out the raspy breathing of a three pack a day smoker close to her ear. His fetid breath, a mixture of ashes and stale alcohol, almost made her gag.

"Get down on your knees," he ordered and she felt the barrel of a gun push into the back of her neck.

With legs that felt as stable as a plate of Jell-O, she fell rather than lowered herself to the ground as she mentally scrambled to place the voice of the attacker. Behind her she heard him press numbers into a mobile phone. Would he kill her here or was he calling for further instructions? Would there be an opportunity to escape if he took her to another location?

"I have her." In the silence she heard the low hum of an air conditioner unit nearby, the rumble of a truck out on the street, her own heartbeat tapping out a quickstep in her ears.

"I understand."

The phone call disconnected and she clenched her teeth in frustration. So much for gaining any insight with that conversation.

"I have a message for you," the ominous voice informed her. "Mister Spiros says he looks forward to seeing you real soon."

The floor seemed to roll beneath her knees and she blinked to clear the veil of dots that had appeared before her eyes. They'd found her. After all her hard work to stay invisible, they'd somehow managed to track her down.

The last thing she remembered was his nasty, phlegmy chuckle before she felt a blow to her head and hit the floor in a painful heap.

* * * *

As expected, Tully lashed out the moment she opened her eyes.

One hand on the wheel, Jake did his best to calm her. "Tully, it's okay. You're safe."

Sharply, she turned her head. Jake kept one eye on the night road before him and one arm across her chest to help settle her down. Waking up restrained by the seat belt couldn't have been fun.

"Where are we? What happened?" she croaked, her voiced sounding raw and painful in the cabin of his four-wheel drive. "How did I get here?"

"I heard your car pull up and went outside just in time to see some guy grab you and push you inside. It's okay, he can't hurt you anymore."

Jake hadn't waited around to find out if the guy he'd knocked out had been working alone. There wasn't time. He'd just run upstairs, grabbed a handful of clothing from Tully's wardrobe, the first set of shoes he'd laid his hands on, made a sweep through the kitchen to grab her Glock and ammo, then shoved the whole lot into her running-clothes bag before placing Tully into the passenger seat of his four-wheel drive and leaving town.

She'd been asleep for the last two hours. He'd kept a vigilant check on her, thinking at least his medic training had come in handy for something. Although he knew she was okay, he was breathing a lot easier now that she'd opened her eyes.

"I can protect you, but you have to trust me. I know you're a good detective and you've kept yourself safe up until now. You can't do this alone anymore."

"You think I don't know what they're capable of?"

He glanced toward her and saw she sat with her arms wrapped tight around her middle. A strong urge to comfort her swelled up inside him but she wasn't looking at all receptive to any comforting at the moment. He had to admire that in her.

"I know a place we can go to and you'll be safe. Close your eyes, Tully, and let me do the worrying for a little while. You need to rest."

She didn't look as though she could summon the energy to protest, and he watched as her eyes fluttered closed and she drifted back into what had to be an exhausted sleep.

* * * *

Tully took a deep breath as she slid into her bulletproof vest and rechecked her gun. Her eyes felt like sandpaper from the long night of briefing and planning the big assault. She was past exhaustion though. A twenty-minute nap two hours ago had revitalized her enough. Adrenaline began to pump through her veins as the squad prepared to raid the Spiros family mansion and search for the evidence she had been able to supply during her six months undercover inside the family.

She had asked to be included in the raid, needing to see this through to the end. Normally undercover police would be sheltered, protected, even arrested along with the criminals in order to protect their identity, but Tully wasn't in the undercover unit. This was a onetime job she'd signed on for. Afterward, she would be free to return to her previous life, clear of this mess, and be able to put it to rest.

Doors slammed inside the warehouse-like shed the unit worked from. Engines started and carefully cars, vans, and a tactical response truck convoyed out into the dark predawn Melbourne morning.

The trip was tense. Tully was focused on the job ahead and eager to have it finished.

The raid went off according to plan—the tactical response guys going in first. Tully went in with the second wave and headed for the office and a secure room in back of the house where she knew the business dealings were conducted and most of the physical evidence would be located. The information they found there would lead the squad to the location of a vast drug and weapons cache, taking out a major supply chain which serviced the majority of the east coast of Australia.

Walking back through the house, she went in search of the man she'd set out to destroy. A mixture of anger, pride, and relief boiled inside her as she approached Leo Spiros, seated, hands cuffed and watching her approach with eyes full of venom and loathing.

Standing before him, she was the complete opposite of the slinky-dressed creature he had fallen head over heels with six months prior. She saw the shock in his eyes as he registered the identity of the female cop standing before him. His mouth dropped open and his eyes bulged in disbelief.

"Georgia?"

She narrowed her eyes at the name he'd crooned in her ear for six months and allowed for the first time the hate she felt for this man to flow freely. "Leo Spiros, you are under arrest for the possession and sale of illegal arms and drugs."

"I don't understand...you can't..."

She continued to read him his rights, ignoring his growing agitation, trying desperately to keep the shake of delayed reaction from her voice. Hold it together, Tully. It's not over yet. Don't let this piece of crap see how much he's taken away from you.

"Who are you?" he demanded, almost hysterical.

"I'm the partner of Detective Senior Constable Wade Spencer, the man you killed in cold blood a little over six months ago. Do you remember him?" she asked, walking toward him slowly, her intense gaze pinning him. "He left behind a wife and child. He was also my best friend. That's who I am, and I wish I could do more than throw you in prison for drug and arms possession, but we both know who killed him, don't we, Leo?"

His eyes lost the look of madness, but in its place a cold, dangerous expression descended, one that sent a chill down her back.

"I don't know what you're talking about, Detective, and I think I should have my lawyer here before you start making accusations like that."

"I hope you rot in hell, you spineless piece of crap." She held *his stare for a few moments then turned and walked away. "Was nice knowing you, Leo."*

Chapter Eight

Tully's eyes snapped open and she sat up quickly in her seat, shaking the lingering memories from her mind. Sunlight was shining in the window and the scenery was now completely different. Endless brown plains of nothingness stretched out, broken here and there by large barren hills rising out of the earth like molehills.

Docile-looking Brahmans stood under whatever form of shade they could find in their paddocks alongside the road, staring off into the distance with blank expressions. The shimmering heat, refracting across the road in the distance, distorted the image of the horizon as far as she could see.

Jake took his attention from the road long enough to send her a lazy grin. "Hello, sleeping beauty."

"I didn't mean to fall asleep." She stared at the clock on the dash of the car and realized she'd been asleep for hours. She blinked in surprise. When was the last time she had managed to sleep for so long?

"You were exhausted," he said with a shrug.

Tully let her gaze wander over his profile. He hadn't shaved and the stubble on his face made him look more than a little dangerous. She watched his big, capable hands on the steering wheel and felt almost...safe.

Get a grip, Chambers. Safe is not the word you should be using around this man.

Jake had already proven he could find holes in her defenses, and she seemed unable to defend herself against him. It was almost more exhausting trying to keep an eye on him than on the Spiros family.

Tully glanced over her shoulder into the back of the tightly packed four-wheel drive. There seemed to be enough equipment there for a six-month camping expedition. "How long has this been planned for? Seems like you should be pretty exhausted too," she offered dryly.

"I'm okay. I've had plenty of practice staying awake," he assured her. "I decided yesterday when you were at work it might be time to get you out of town for a while. Things kinda got pushed forward when your friend decided to knock you over the head."

"You didn't by any chance have something to do with last night, did you?" The sudden thought formed in her head. "Get someone to give me a scare in order to make me leave?"

He swivelled an incredulous glance in her direction. "Yeah, Chambers, I set up the whole thing just to get you alone, complete with almost giving you a concussion."

"Okay." She admitted how paranoid she sounded with a grimace. "That was a stupid question."

An angry, brittle silence filled the space between them inside the cabin of the vehicle. "You've been under a lot of stress," he conceded, but his tone still held a clipped, almost injured sound to it.

"I'm sorry I accused you of setting me up, but don't patronize me. I can deal with stress. I'm not some delicate little princess who needs a big strong man to shield her from life's unpleasantness."

He lowered his head in assent. His lips twitched. "My mistake. Stress was obviously the wrong word. Maybe shock would be a better one."

Tully gritted her teeth. She couldn't stand being patted on the head and sent away like a child, and hated even more when men made her out to be some kind of man-hating feminist if she objected to the manner in which they spoke to her.

"Well, shock or no shock, I need a coffee."

Reaching down beside his chair, he handed over a polystyrene cup with a black lid. "I figured you would."

Tully's mouth dropped open but she reached out to take the cup from his hand. Was there no end to this man's ability to be one step ahead of her?

"Where are we headed?" she asked between tentative sips. "Or is that information too far out of my scope of understanding?"

Jake ignored her jibe. "A friend of mine offered a place up north for a few of us to use whenever we needed to get back to nature."

"Back to nature...Why don't I like the sound of that?" she asked with a tingle of dread.

"Come on, Tully, you don't seem the kind of woman who'd be put off by the lack of a few of life's luxuries," he said, sending her a challenging look.

"Expand on the lack of luxuries thing," she said cautiously.

"There's a house and running water."

"Where is this fabulous retreat we're going to?"

"Let's just say we won't be getting there today."

Tully looked at the road ahead which ran straight for who knew how many kilometers. "Well, I guess they'll never think of looking this far out of civilization," she murmured.

"We won't be taking that for granted. Grab some food out of the cooler behind your seat if you're hungry." As if on cue her stomach rumbled and Tully groaned in embarrassment. Jake's chuckle echoed close to her ear in the confined space of the car but she ignored him and reached back to see what he'd packed to eat. Seemed they were in for a very long trip.

Later in the afternoon, Tully switched with Jake to give him a rest. He gave her the map in case she got lost but even though his eyes were closed she sensed he was somehow aware of everything she was doing. It should have felt creepy but instead was kind of comforting.

As night fell, quite late, Jake pulled into a small clearing off the main road and set up camp for the night.

They made a small fire and she sat back while Jake set about cooking a surprisingly tasty meal on his compact army stove. As darkness descended upon them, the open desert landscape became cooler.

Tully looked out into the shadows and shivered. She felt so small and insignificant. Who would miss them if they were murdered and left for dead out here? she wondered listlessly. Jake, who had his mates, more like brothers, would be mourned. The prosecution would be...

Annoyed, their last witness a no-show. Her gaze lowered to the enamel mug she held between her hands and realized just how alone she really was. Even Aunt Norma, the mean old witch, had died within the last year, leaving Tully with...no one.

"That mug could tell some stories."

She glanced up at Jake, reclining against a box nearby, watching her with a steady, intense gaze. "This mug?"

He dropped his focus to the cup in her hand, with chipped enamel and the odd dent on the side. "It's been with me on every tour, every exercise and every near miss I've ever had."

She smiled as she pictured the battered mug hanging from a heavy backpack, through bush and desert, rain and drought. "You miss the army." Her observation came from the wistful expression on his face as he fell back into memories of the past.

"Yeah, I do. I guess I miss the mateship and the belonging to something the most. It's hard to get used to civilian life when you've been in the army for as long as I have, but I miss the company more than the job, I think."

She envied that about his job. She remembered a time when she'd felt the same of her own career, but somewhere along the line the camaraderie, as well as her social life, had seemed to fizzle out. There just didn't seem to be enough time to fit anything in except work. Maybe she should have taken time out to have a life, but the drive to succeed had made everything else seem unimportant.

"No family?" Damn it. Why had she asked that?

"None to speak of." He gave a small shrug of one large shoulder. "My dad remarried when I was a kid and had a new family, but he never kept in touch. Haven't seen him since I was eight. It was just Mum and me until she died the year after I enlisted. How about you?"

Two more things they had in common. Fathers who had abandoned them and mothers who had died young. If Tully hadn't been so exhausted, she might have mustered the strength to keep her walls intact. Instead, the food, the warmth of the fire, the quiet companionship of the man who seemed determined to insert himself into her life relaxed her enough to say, "No one. I only had my mum as well but she was...she died when I was fifteen, and I...I went to live with my mother's older sister."

Jake shifted, getting more comfortable, and she felt her spirits dampen. He was settling in for the long haul and she was going to have to start exposing her sordid past.

"Do I detect a lack of affection for this aunty of yours?" he asked, hitching an eyebrow curiously.

"Let's just say getting lumped with a hormonal, slightly jaded fifteen-year-old was probably the last thing a God-fearing Christian spinster in her late sixties would have wanted or expected," Tully admitted dryly, "but being the good Christian she was, she couldn't say no." She glanced Jake's way, but quickly turned to the fire instead. She wasn't sure what she wanted to see in his eyes, or how she would feel if she did—or didn't find it. Suddenly she felt as confused as that hormonal fifteen-year-old she'd once been. "No, there wasn't a great deal of love lost between us. She gave up on me a long time ago."

The crickets chirped loudly between them as Tully stared into the glow of the fire, taking comfort where she could.

"Not everyone gives up that easy, Tully," Jake said quietly.

She lifted her attention from the cheerful crackle of the campfire to Jake. The light flickered and cast shadows across his features but she felt his steady gaze holding her own.

"Maybe in your world they don't, Jake, but in mine they do."

"We've already established you're no longer in your world, Chambers." He grinned. "Food for thought."

With that, he tossed the dregs of his coffee into the darkness behind him and got to his feet. A tent had been set up already, and as Tully broke into a jaw-breaking yawn, Jake retrieved two sleeping bags from the rear of his car.

"Come on, Cinderella, time to turn in."

Too tired to put up any kind of protest at this point, she followed him into the little dome tent, which was unexpectedly cozy and quite warm.

"I'll be back once I've taken care of the fire and checked everything."

Sliding in between the sleeping bag's space-age-looking material, she squirmed to get comfortable and listened to the sounds of Jake moving about outside. A smile touched her lips. It was nice to have someone to help carry the load. This wasn't her turf. Alone in the city, she'd be fine. She'd been trained to fit in and adapt to situations, to take care of herself. Out here, though, was a whole different ball game. This was Jake's domain. She hoped he knew what he was doing, because her life pretty much depended upon it.

The flap of the tent opened and she heard the zip closing them safely inside. A strange attack of butterflies exploded within her. Giving herself a mental slap she pushed away the silly schoolgirl reaction, determined to regather the cool woman of the world façade she felt more comfortable with.

Jake gave a frustrated sigh as she continued to toss and turn in her sleeping bag, then without warning reached over and dragged her bag closer. With deft fingers he unzipped and fitted the two bags together. "Now, lay still and get to sleep, Chambers."

Too shocked to react at first, it did occur to her that she should protest, but the warmth which spread with delicious speed from his body to hers changed her mind. With a full stomach, a warm bed, and the heavy comfort of a man's arm draped across her hip protectively, it was almost too easy to forget that somewhere out there, somebody wanted her very dead.

Chapter Nine

By midday they were on a dusty red dirt road, still in the middle of nowhere.

"Are we there yet?" she asked halfheartedly.

"Almost," Jake said, giving her a quick smile.

She sat a little straighter and looked around with a renewed interest.

"Just another few hundred kilometers and we'll be there," he added cheerfully.

The sheer frustration of having endured so many miles was taking its toll on her usual good nature. To have the optimistic hope of arrival snatched from beneath her feet like that was almost enough to bring her to tears.

They'd stopped at small towns for gas along the way, some not even towns, just portable buildings no bigger than a caravan with a few groceries and a single gas pump. Tully made sure she took full advantage of each stop to stretch her legs and unkink tired muscles while Jake scanned their surroundings with unwavering vigilance. He kept her within sight at all times, even going as far as to wait outside the ladies, until Tully put a stop to it, pointing out she was more than capable of going to the toilet without his assistance. She'd won at least that one small battle.

It continued to amaze her that he was able to function so well on such limited sleep. His years of training were still obviously very much a part of his nature.

They filled in the countless hours of travel with conversation. He told her about his time in the army and amused her with tales from his training camp days, and situations that made her laugh, and at other times, made her feel like crying. Over those few days, confined in their tiny cocoon of isolation, Tully had time, without the intrusion of everyday life, to gain a deeper understanding of the man beside her. She discovered a depth within him she had not expected.

She'd already known, in their limited time spent together, that he posed a considerable threat to her well-being. Alone with him now, spending every waking moment together, she was certain Jake Holden was potentially just as much of a threat to her life as the people she was running from. He might not want her dead, which made him the lesser of the two evils, but did he want something from her that would ultimately mean the end of her life...as she now knew it.

She took comfort in the knowledge that at least with Jake she might still have the energy to walk away from him after all this was over. That because of him and the security he offered, she *would* be able to walk away and this was the trade-off she had to make.

The roads became more deteriorated the closer they came to their final destination. The scenery was the same—red dirt, scrubby trees and very little else to see. They crossed a cattle grid. Jake sat a little higher in his seat.

"This is it."

They drove along a dusty track that seemed to go on forever, until it swept around a bend and there in front of them was a small cluster of buildings. Large machinery sheds circled a smaller building that looked to be the main house. The roof had rusted and the steps at the front of the house had sagged, leading onto a front veranda that looked as though it might actually be falling away from the rest of the house. Its timber walls were a mournful shade of grey, a legacy of the generations of exposure to harsh elements without the benefit of fresh paint.

"Wow, this is...rustic," Tully said, getting out of the car and pushing her gas-station-bought new sunglasses onto the top of her head.

"A real fixer-upper," Jake agreed with a lopsided grin, "but it'll do the job."

"I thought you said it had running water." Tully turned an accusing look toward Jake.

"There is, especially in winter. You have to *run* real fast down to the creek to get a bucket of water and back to the house before you freeze." He chuckled at her grimace but kept walking toward the front door to inspect their dwellings.

Tully sighed and followed him with all the enthusiasm of a woman being led to the gallows.

A man walked from behind the sheds toward them and she tensed, then relaxed, as Jake shouted a welcome.

"It's okay," Jake assured her with a warm grin. "He's one of ours."

Jake's reassurance did little to set her mind at rest though. She'd spent too long not trusting anyone but herself. The two men shook hands and shared a grin of camaraderie. They exchanged a few words, and then Tully watched as the stranger turned and jogged away.

Jake shot her a glance as he began to unpack their gear. "You're going to have to trust me on this, Chambers. I don't need an army of men out here to keep you safe, but I would trust my life and yours with the few I do have, so give me a hand to unload this stuff, will you?"

He just didn't realize how momentous the simple task of trusting was for her. It seemed she had little choice in the matter however. Here, in the back of beyond, she was going to need Jake and whoever else he had roped into helping them, and that was all there was to it.

The inside wasn't falling apart as badly as the outside, which was saying a lot. There was very little furniture and a few stray cobwebs in the far corners of the ceiling, but at least there weren't any cracks in the walls and creepy crawlies taking up residence... none that she could see anyway.

Jake spotted her standing in the center of the room with her hands on her hips. Turning in a slow circle she inspected the room with an expression that could only be described as pained.

"Yeah, I know it's not the Hyatt," he said, "but we need a place that's not easy to access and that we can lay low in."

"Well, this is the right place to be then. It's all that...and more," she agreed dryly, but softened her sarcasm with a small smile. "It's the perfect place to be right now. Thanks, Jake, for doing all this. It's above and beyond the neighborly thing to do. I know I haven't been exactly appreciative over the last few days. I just want you to know I am though...grateful." She felt self-conscious and out of her element here in the middle of nowhere with a man she was beginning to like way too much.

"You're more than welcome, but trust me, Tully, there's nothing neighborly about my intentions," he said with a wink, leaving before she could comment.

Once the gear had been unpacked, Jake suggested she go and have a bath.

"A bath? You've waited until *now* to tell me this place has a *bath*?"

He flashed a brief smile. "Well, I wouldn't have gotten any work out of you if I told you that up front, would I?" He led her toward the rear of the house and opened a door to a bathroom, complete with a claw-footed bathtub in the center of the room.

Taking a candle from the sink, he lit and placed it by the tub, then turned on the spigots and fiddled with them until he was satisfied.

"I will warn you, the hot water system hasn't kicked in yet, but it's warm. Best I could do with short notice." He shrugged. "There's an outside shower if you would prefer," he said with a straight face.

"Think I'll take my chances with the tub, thanks." *Thank God,* Tully thought, closing her eyes in relief as Jake handed her a towel and left her to it, *there is running water after all!*

She stepped from her clothes and eased into the tepid water. A sigh of pleasure escaped as she lowered herself into the tub and the water crept inch by inch up her weary body.

She listened to the trickling of the water as it ran through her fingers. Cupping her hands, she scooped the water and let it dribble over her face. After washing the grime from her travels off her skin, she lay back and watched the candlelight flicker and play across the water. It was almost too easy to close her eyes and pretend she was anywhere but here.

Rubbing her hair dry with a towel, she came out of the bathroom feeling far more human than when she had walked in.

She took her towel out to the veranda and hung it over the rail to dry as she took in the backyard and big sheds before her. She tried to picture it as it would have been when it was a working property and felt sad at the signs of neglect that suggested it had been a long time since this place housed a family. There was no sign of Jake, so she made her way down the veranda to inspect the rest of the place.

A sound caught her attention and she decided to follow it, thinking it would lead her to Jake's whereabouts. Lead to him it did. As she rounded the corner she came to an abrupt stop, unable to force her gaze or legs to move.

Jake stood with his back to her, naked under a stream of water from a showerhead, suspended beneath a large, rusty water tank.

As though sensing her eyes upon him, he turned to face her.

He was magnificent. Wide shoulders tapered down to narrow hips and muscular thighs. The dark hair on his body sleeked with water made him glisten in the setting sun's last rays of light.

He blinked beneath the water and, in a slow, unhurried movement, raised his arms to wipe the water from his face. The man was every lurid fantasy she'd ever had, come to life.

Reaching above his head and exposing the dark hair beneath his arms, so male and arousing, he tugged at a rope and the water stopped falling.

As though the act had enabled her brain to suddenly function, she caught her breath and turned to hurry back toward the house. She paced back and forth in the kitchen, appalled by her open ogling of the man. What was she? Desperate? Yes, they had slept together, but this was different. So much had happened since then. He knew her fears, her secrets, and had seen her at her lowest. It was different now.

What had she done? Stood there and stared at him like a hungry animal. Like she'd never seen a naked man before.

You haven't, her lust-filled brain yelled back at her. *Not built like that!*

Even so, she covered her face, mortified. What on earth was she going to say to him when they eventually came face to face once more?

Chapter Ten

Jake's quiet chuckle caught her off guard and she dropped her hands to look up. "I'm sorry. I didn't know you were there."

A self-conscious grin touched his mouth and he shook his head. "It's okay. I should have warned you I was going to have a shower. I just hope I didn't scare you too badly, or steal your appetite," he added with a slight bitterness she suspected he directed at his burn wounds.

Was he serious? "It didn't scare me or turn me off...anything." Her voice sounded breathless to her ears and he snapped his gaze up to search her eyes.

Her shirt felt too tight and her breathing became labored. He'd pulled on his jeans and T-shirt but hadn't bothered drying himself and wet marks were soaking through his shirt.

She could smell the clean fresh smell of the soap he'd just used beneath the heady fragrance of prime male. Swallowing nervously, she forced herself to stand still as he lifted a hand toward her face to cup her jaw. Her eyes fluttered closed at the surge of desire that ran through her from his touch. Opening them, she made a decision. Leaning forward, she met his lips in a hot, hungry kiss that drew a rugged groan from Jake. He lifted her to sit on the kitchen counter, bringing them to the same height.

Her position brought her to eye level with him and she wiggled forward to wrap her legs around his waist. The movement drew him tight against her and she could feel the hard length of him pushing through the worn fabric of his jeans.

Never had Tully lost control the way she was losing it now. The feeling was frightening, terrifying in its intensity, but also incredibly intoxicating. A wanton, lustful aching deep within that demanded to be released.

Running her hands up his arms, across the wide, powerful shoulders, she found her way into his spiky crop of hair, where she scraped her nails along his scalp, drowning in the heady power of their attraction to one another.

Releasing his hold, he slid one hand from her hip to her leg, inching toward the junction of her thighs. When he reached it, she let out a shattered, jagged sigh that sent a ripple of delight through her entire body. She groaned in frustration when her body craved more of him.

"You're wearing too many clothes," she told him, her voice raspy with awakened desire.

"I can fix that." Within moments he'd tugged his T-shirt over his head and kicked off his jeans, standing naked before her once more and looking pleased with himself.

They shared a chuckle before the blazing need erased the gentle humor between them. Slowly she crossed her arms before her, grabbed the bottom of her shirt and pulled it up over her head, then dropped it to the floor.

She watched his gaze travel across the smooth skin of her torso, feasting with hungry eyes on the swell of her breasts, encased in white lace and satin.

Reaching behind, she unhooked the bra and let it fall to the ground to join the steadily growing pile of clothing at their feet.

With reverent awe, he cupped a breast in each hand, and rubbed her sensitive nipples with calloused thumbs. His eyes darkened in appreciation at her lustful sighs and electric response.

Arching into his touch, she demanded more and squeezed her legs tighter around his waist, drawing him closer. She gave a long low moan of ecstasy as she felt his warm lips take one hardened peak in his mouth and swirl his tongue in a mind-blowing assault on her senses.

With an urgent need pulsing through her veins, she helped him tug the rest of her clothing off, and with only minimal probing to ensure she was satisfactorily ready, he entered her in one smooth, slow stroke.

Their twin moans of rapture were swallowed in a savage kiss fuelled by the intensity of their passion. Tully matched him thrust for thrust, throwing her head back in abandon, as the smell of lust and sweat and sex filled the room, making her dizzy with need.

Their climaxes came swift and violent, like a majestic force of nature, leaving them breathless and weak in its wake.

Gathering his strength, Jake plucked her from the counter and carried her toward the bedroom he'd put her belongings in earlier, depositing her gently on the creaky old bed.

Struggling to raise herself up onto her elbows, she eyed him curiously as he stood at the base of the bed, looking tall, proud, and incredibly sexy.

"What? That's it?" she teased. "That's all you've got?"

His eyes narrowed and he flashed her a wolf-like grin. "Lady, you ain't seen nothin' yet," he promised before joining her on the bed, causing the mattress to protest not unlike Aunty Norma on one of her rants.

* * * *

Tully found Jake sitting on the edge of the veranda in back of the house when she ventured outdoors much later that evening. She stepped out the doorway and eased herself down beside him.

A sagging fence divided the house yard from the endless plains that seemed to stretch toward the horizon. Small bushy trees dotted the barren landscape. The sun was setting and the sky looked as though it were on fire. The deep reds, browns, and terra-cottas splashed the earth and seemed to vibrate across the land.

"Wow, the sunsets here are breathtaking," Tully murmured, unable to drag her eyes from nature's amazing display before them

"Not too shabby," Jake agreed.

"Who is this mysterious friend who owns this place?"

"He's a retired army brigadier and a good friend. This property has been in his family for generations, but they've all long gone. He chose a career in the army over farming and after his parents died the property went to him. He can't bring himself to sell it off, so it just sits here to be used whenever anyone needs to get away from it all."

"Or hide out from irate mob bosses," she added with a strange lightness she wouldn't have thought possible before coming here.

"Or that," he agreed with a smile. "Hungry?" he asked, dragging the cooler toward him to open the lid.

"Sure. What culinary delights do you have hidden away in there?"

He handed her a plastic-wrapped sandwich and a cold beer, then reached in and withdrew his own.

Tully was starving. Their marathon of sex had reinstated a hunger she hadn't felt in a long time.

On more than one level.

"You know people would pay a fortune to dine with a view like this," she said between bites of her chicken sandwich.

"Only the best for you, Tully," he said, clinking his beer can against her own in a toast.

"Ah, there was something I wanted to bring up though...We didn't use anything, back in the kitchen...I can't believe I lost my head like that and forgot all about it." He winced and lifted his eyes to her face uncomfortably. "Do you think that's going to be a...problem?"

Tully gave a small chuckle. "It's okay. I'm on the pill—and I have a clean bill of health, in case you're worried," she added dryly.

He let out a long sigh of relief and shook his head. "It wasn't catching anything I was worried about." At her cocked eyebrow he rubbed one large hand across the back of his neck awkwardly. "I've seen firsthand the effect an unwanted pregnancy can have on people. I wouldn't wish the kind of relationship my parents had on any kid."

Thinking back to her own screwed-up family, she had to admit he had a point—kids paid the price for mistakes their parents made.

She regarded him while she chewed, as he took a long sip of his beer, watching his strong neck muscles working, and felt those pesky butterflies as they fluttered against her rib cage again.

"It must take a lot of guts to work undercover," he commented as he set the empty can down beside him, changing the topic.

She was surprised by his conversation choice but, out in this isolated place, she felt safe for the first time in a very long time. "I don't usually work undercover. I was just an ordinary detective in the wrong place at the right time."

"What happened?" Jake asked between bites of his sandwich.

"I bumped into Leonardo Spiros at a club one night. I had been following him for a while, working out a way to get something on him. I didn't realize an active task force had also been working him and his father at the same time." Her smile was tinged with sarcasm. "They asked me to cooperate with the task force, go undercover legitimately, through Leo, and gather intel on his father and the business. The rest is history." She shrugged.

"Why were you following him in the first place?" Jake asked, wearing a frown.

"He killed my partner...and got off. I couldn't just let him walk away. I figured if I could get him *and* bring down the rest of his corrupt family while I was at it, then all the better." She stared into the depths of the beer can she held in her hand.

"Was it hard to do...pretend to like the guy even though you hated his guts?"

"Understatement. At first I was worried I wouldn't be able to be in the same room with him without killing him, then...I don't know, I thought to myself, why not make the bastard pay?"

"He never suspected?"

She lifted her gaze to stare out into the endless landscape before them and gave a snort of contempt. "Men like Leo..." Tully's voice faded out as she remembered the ruthless cruelty that had lain under his charming persona. "No, he never did."

"Did you begin to have feelings for him?" Jake's quiet question surprised her.

"No." She blinked away unpleasant memories. "It didn't take a psychologist to figure out the father was a manipulative bastard who got his kicks screwing with his kid's head. I guess in a way it made it easier to...get close to him and make it realistic. I tried not to think too much about it one way or the other. I was just doing a job."

Jake went quiet and Tully forced herself to look up and meet his gaze. A sinking feeling crossed her mind that he was too quiet. "Thinking twice about that warning to stay away from me now, aren't you?" She tipped the last of her beer down her throat and swallowed.

"I warned you that uncovering my secrets was something you didn't want to mess with. You should have listened when I warned you the first time." She stood up and looked down at his big frame, elbows braced along the length of his thighs, hands clasped loose between his knees, and felt a strange sensation she hadn't felt before...*hurt*. His reaction, the fact that he refused to meet her eyes, hurt her feelings like nothing had been able to hurt her in a very long time.

"You didn't mention how you got your evidence against the family before." Jake's tone held a slight tinge of defensiveness and he still wouldn't look at her.

"How did you think undercover works?" she asked, exasperated. When he didn't comment she turned and walked away. As she reached the door fury rose up inside her and she turned back to face him. "What bugs you more, Jake," she asked, her voice as harsh as the unforgiving land around them, "that the damsel you're determined to save isn't snow-white, or that you just didn't want to believe it?"

"Just tell me one thing, Tully, *honestly*." He stressed the word and Tully felt as though he had slapped her. "How do I know if you were telling me the truth when you said you weren't feeling sorry for me?"

Tully stared at him, dumbfounded, her injured feelings taking a back seat to this new and, decidedly worse, feeling of shame.

What else was he supposed to think? She'd just told him she'd conned a man into a relationship to get information from him. Why would he trust anything she'd told him after hearing that?

A horrible rush of humiliation washed over her as always, whenever she made the mistake of thinking too long about the case. She felt dirty and manipulative. Of course, deep down she knew she'd done what she had to do and that the circumstances were hardly black-and-white, but to be judged by her past, and have her actions questioned now, stung a little. Who was she kidding? It stung a lot!

"You got me, Jake. I guess sometimes I blur the line between my job and my personal life. Of course I felt sorry for you. Of course I'd throw myself at you to make you feel less humiliated about your scars, all the while laughing at you behind your back."

The need to hide from the humiliation and self-loathing was so volatile within, it threatened to explode and taint everything around her. Reefing open the screen door, she stormed through the house and changed into something easier to run in. Letting the door slam behind her, she ignored Jake still seated alone on the edge of the veranda.

She pushed her way through the overgrown bush along the fence line—once planted and tended with love, but now abandoned and left to overrun the yard—and headed for the dirt road they'd driven in on. Blood pumped through her body as her feet pounded the ground, sending small puffs of dust up behind her, the need to distance herself from the farmhouse and the man still back there powering her stride.

A branch scratched across her face as she brushed too close to where it overhung the track but Tully ignored the sting, glad to be able to focus on physical pain for a change. It was far easier to deal with than the emotional pain she'd been experiencing of late.

Faster and faster she ran, until the wind stole away the tears that had begun to fall. Never had she cried so often, in such a short time span. She never cried! Not since she'd run away from Aunt Norma. Besides, it was counterproductive and a waste of energy.

Ever since Jake Holden had barged into her life, this annoying weakness had seemed to resurface.

She'd been judged by her past too many times to count. Her aunt Norma had prayed unceasingly for her deprived soul, having lived with a mother who went through men like most people went through underwear. Then by her colleagues, who'd dug into her history and presented her with an embarrassing file full of credentials they'd claimed made her perfect for working undercover.

Her two years spent on the street when dear Aunt Norma had decided her soul was damned for eternity—after Tully had argued with the church minister Norma had sent for to counsel her on the evil of her teenage ways—had apparently caught their eye. A spate of juvenile pickups for alleged prostitution had apparently made her the perfect candidate for worming a path into Leo Spiros's life.

She'd learned years ago people tended to assume alleged was the same as convicted and no longer wasted her breath defending herself. She knew she'd gotten by on the streets by her wits and her ability to read people, a skill she'd honed through years of weighing up the men her mother had brought home. It had earned her a reputation amongst her coworkers for knowing exactly which technique would break which criminal.

Her brush with the law at a young age hadn't been all bad though. She'd met a detective who had worked her mother's murder case, and a chance meeting years later had been the catalyst for her choice of a career in the police force. As she liked to think of it, with a smirk as she thought of her aunt Norma, using her powers for good and not for evil. She could have gone either way had it not been for that one insightful detective.

One who reminded her a lot of Spence. Spence. The reason she was here with Jake today.

After a while she began to tire and turned back. She slowed her pace to a comfortable jog and then to a walk as she cooled down. Jake stood like a silent sentry on the front porch, watching her progress back up the driveway. Tully ignored him, brushing by without a word—the noisy squeak of the rusty hinges on the door the only sound that passed between them as she headed for the bathroom to wash the sweat and dust from her blood-smeared face.

Staring at the image in the old bathroom mirror, its gilded edges corroded and faded with age, she told her reflection she didn't care what he thought of her. By the time she had cleaned up Tully had almost convinced herself she believed it.

The house was dark but not silent. She laid out the sleeping bag Jake had packed for her in the living room, which was situated in the very center of the building. She refused to sleep in the bed where only a few short hours ago they had shared the most amazing sex she'd ever experienced.

Jake waited until she was settled before he came into the room and set up his own sleeping bag close to the doorway. Tully listened to the house's strange creaks and groans, the sound of corrugated iron cracking and clicking as the heat of the day eased and the temperature outside cooled down.

She hadn't spoken a word to him since returning. What was there to say? He had, without a doubt, made up his mind about her and would be keeping his distance from now on, exactly what she had wanted in the first place.

It didn't explain, though, why she felt as though she had lost something irreplaceable.

Chapter Eleven

When Tully awoke the next morning, Jake's sleeping bag was empty. It was warm, even at this early hour, a sign they were in for a long, hot day. Tully splashed her face with water in the bathroom, and eyed the scratch across her cheek. *Just superficial,* she thought, *almost healed...*and yet she still felt the sting.

Sunlight streamed through the front windows and Tully wandered outdoors to sit on one of the two old cane chairs that sat on either side of a weather-beaten square table, and sipped at the cup of steaming coffee she'd made before going outside.

She could hear noise coming from one of the large machinery sheds across the yard and solved the mystery of Jake's whereabouts. *Good,* she thought to herself, he was out of the way and she would be able to go ahead and do what she now realized had to be done in order to bring this all to an end.

Tully dug out her mobile and prayed she'd find a signal. With a small sigh of relief she saw that three of the bars indicating reception stared back from the small screen. She dialled the number and waited for it to connect and ring. A glimmer of a smile touched her lips as a familiar, impatient "Yes?" greeted her.

There was nothing that could be mistaken as congenial about her boss or, for that matter, instantly likeable. She'd put more than one person off with her direct manner and wasted little time with niceties. Louise Bollinger, or—as she was more commonly known in the job by the majority of her male colleagues—Ball-Buster-Bollinger was not someone you messed with. Even they, however, had to admire and respect the woman for her professionalism.

"Hello, Louise. It's Tully," she said, and heard the line go silent for a heartbeat before the older woman seemed to recover from her surprise.

"Well, well, well, the prodigal daughter returns at long last." Tully guessed by the dry greeting that her task force encounter had not gone down well with her boss.

"I know." Tully sighed. "I have a lecture coming, but not right now, Louise. I'm calling because I want to come back to work."

"You don't think that's a tad premature?"

"I'm sick of these people dictating my life. I want to go back to work until the trial."

"After all this time, now I'm reliable enough to call on, to get you out of trouble?" Louise asked in her abrupt, scornful manner.

"Louise, now is not the time to become irrational."

Tully heard an irritated sigh on the other end before Louise demanded, "Where do you want to meet?"

"I'll let you know once I have a few things in place."

Tully ended the call and sat looking at her phone as she pondered the conversation. She was able to breathe a little easier knowing she would be able to stop running. She just hoped she'd done the right thing, getting her boss involved, and wasn't about to endanger yet another life.

Deciding she needed at least one full cup of fortification inside her before she faced Jake this morning, she sipped at her coffee, savoring its smooth texture.

The rhythmic sound of filing greeted her as she cautiously entered the large grey shed a few minutes later. Hay bales were stacked along one side. They appeared to have been there for quite some time, looking anything but appetizing. Then again, she was no hay connoisseur and really no judge of what might or might not be considered fine fodder.

Jake was standing side on to a large vice when she walked across the shed to stand beside him. He didn't lift his head but she knew from the way his body tensed he was aware she was there.

"What are you doing?" she asked after a few moments when she realized he wasn't about to stop what he was doing to greet her.

"Taking care of a few things around the place. Did you have something else in mind?" he asked in a tone she found difficult to read.

Tully bent to retrieve a stray piece of hay on the floor and twirled it with absent abandon between her fingertips.

Jake slid the file back and forth across the piece of metal in the vice and with each push his biceps bulged and Tully caught the potent tang of man and sweat and earthy machinery. She dragged her gaze away to focus on the busy birds darting in and out of the high roof as they dive-bombed for bugs, and made nests. It was something to keep her wayward thoughts on the straight and narrow and off those which had the potential to lead her down a dangerous path.

"I've been thinking," Tully told him, tossing the piece of hay to the ground and dusting off her hands.

Jake spared her a brief glance but remained silent, waiting for her to continue.

"I've set up a meeting with my boss. I've decided to go back."

Jake stopped filing and stared at her in disbelief. "You did what?"

"I set up a meeting—" She jumped as Jake slammed the file to the workbench and turned to faced her.

"What part of 'I brought you out here to keep you safe' didn't you get?" he demanded.

"Gee, I don't know, maybe the bit where you suddenly seem like my jailer," she snapped back, refusing to back down when he stepped close.

"Jailer? Lady, you're free to walk away at any time. Don't let a little thing like my trying to save your life stop you," he snarled and turned back to his task.

"Fine," she yelled, walking away from him, fuming at how unreasonable he had become. A few minutes later she heard the sound of a revving engine and saw Jake drive away in a rusty old Ute. Her heart lurched, fearing he was leaving her, but she decided he was blowing off steam. Over the next few hours, though, she found herself wandering outside to scan the horizon for any sign of his whereabouts.

When Jake came back the sun was just about ready to set. From the window she watched him cross the yard, turning away as his big boots sounded on the timber veranda outside. She refused to look up as the squeaky back door announced his arrival. Eating the sandwich she'd halfheartedly prepared earlier, she ignored the uncomfortable silence which threatened to drag on forever.

"I'm sorry. Okay?" he said, his voice low and contrite, standing in the small kitchen waiting for her to look at him. Jake sighed. "I said I was sorry. What more do you want?"

"I want," Tully said as she put her sandwich down on the chipped plate before her, "you to stop jumping in and taking over. I'm quite capable of making my own decisions. I've been a police officer for the last fifteen years and I've been trained well. I may not have been in a war zone, but out there in the streets, every day, there are people who want to kill cops. We walk into situations daily where it's possible that, on the other side of the door, someone is waiting for us with a gun."

Jake drew in a deep breath and nodded his head. "I guess sometimes I forget you can take care of yourself." He considered her as if seeing her in a different light. "You trust her?" Jake asked, going back to their earlier disagreement, staring at Tully hard from his position at the sink.

Tully dropped her gaze to the forlorn, half-eaten sandwich on the plate. "She's been like a mentor to me for the last few years. I've had no reason not to trust her."

"She approve of you going undercover?" He sounded skeptical.

"She didn't know. The task force handled all the arrangements. They told her I was on stress leave and she was given a replacement for me until further notice. I can only imagine how unimpressed she would have been over that." Having thought back over their conversation, Tully knew *exactly* how unimpressed her boss had been.

"They kept her out of the loop as well?" Jake asked with a frown, clearly baffled at how they ran things in the police force.

Tully wiped her hands on a paper napkin as she answered, "No one outside the task force knew anything. That's how they work. Afterward, I didn't get a chance to speak to her directly. Two detectives from the case had been shot. I was told to lay low until the trial was over." Tully went quiet as she thought back over that chaotic time.

"I'm not too excited about calling anyone in on this. The fewer people who know where we are, the better, but it's your decision."

"The sooner this is over the better." A strange flutter in her chest made her stop and think about what she'd just said. It would all be over. She'd be free to leave.

"We wouldn't want it to drag out, would we?" he muttered, turning his back on her to look out over the yard.

She wasn't altogether sure if he was being sarcastic or not. She wouldn't blame him if he really did want to see the back of her as soon as possible.

"I'm sorry about last night. Look," he said, turning to pace in front of her, "I didn't...want you to think that what you told me..." With a frustrated growl he rubbed one big hand across the short hair on his head in frustration.

Tully stared at Jake in surprise.

"I wasn't sure what to say to make you feel better. I should have tried to tell you how I was *feeling*." The last word was accompanied with a grimace, as though tasting weird in his mouth.

She stood and walked toward the sink. Tucking a stray strand of hair behind her ear, she turned to look at him. "I did what was required of me, in order to do a job. It's not who I am. I wasn't lying to you, Jake," she said, reminding him of the question he'd asked her last night about his scars. "I've never lied to you." She gave a small smile at his tiny raised eyebrow. "I may have left out a few details, but I've never lied to you. I didn't sleep with Leo either, in case you were wondering." She saw the self-mocking twist of his lips and added with a shrug, "I just wanted you to know."

He gave a faint nod as he eased himself back against the sink. Strong arms braced his body either side of his hips. "I had no right to judge you, Tully, and I'm sorry I made you feel as though I did."

They were separated by not more than a few feet and, lifting her eyes, she saw that Jake was studying her, his expression solemn. The air seemed to thicken, the distance between them shrank and her body began to tingle with anticipation. Yet neither of them moved.

He took a step closer. The heat radiated between their bodies.

Her hands slid down his waist until they reached the hem of his shirt and she began to lift it. He placed his hands over hers and, for the briefest of moments, Tully thought he was going to stop her. Instead, he helped pull the shirt over his head, his eyes locked onto hers, smoldering desire simmering just below the surface.

She felt his body tremble as she leaned toward him. She pressed her lips against his chest in a light butterfly touch that sent a shudder of emotion through his large frame. When she lifted her eyes to his, she saw they were heavy with desire. As she leaned forward once more, he grabbed her arms and lowered his head to meet her lips in a hungry, desperate kiss.

Desire and longing clawed its way between them. Jake's hands were everywhere, running through her hair, dragging her closer, and pressing her tight against his wide, bare chest.

A buzz sounded and she felt Jake go still. He dragged his mouth from hers with a rugged curse, and she realized it was his phone.

Chapter Twelve

As Jake answered the call, Tully took the opportunity to gather her wits and pull out of his loosened embrace. She saw him frown as she went to the sink, and with unsteady hands, pour a glass of water.

What had she been thinking? She was a day or two at the latest from flying out of here and never seeing Jake again. Why would she even think about doing something as stupid as falling for him at this point in time? *Why?* a little voice asked incredulously. *Just look at him. He's gorgeous. He's saved your life and is here, ready to defend you if the need arises. Why wouldn't you fall for him?*

The voice had an argument, she supposed, but so did the rational side of her brain. The side that calmly pointed out that four thousand plus kilometers was one hell of a commute.

"Sorry, I had to take that," Jake apologized, clearly regretting they had been interrupted.

Tully moved past him to head outside and felt him follow. She was growing quite fond of the back veranda with its spectacular view. The vast, endless plains, the spectacular sunsets, so peaceful and undemanding. Sadly, it would all soon become a distant memory.

"I shouldn't have let things go that far between us. You caught me off guard."

"If it's because of what happened earlier, I've already apologized, and I'm trying to rein in my Neanderthal-man instincts." He sent her a lopsided grin to lighten the mood.

She shook her head. "Jake, all this," she said, waving a hand between them, "just complicates everything. Last night you acted as though I had the plague when you found out about my past, and now that you've discovered I didn't sleep with Leonardo, everything is suddenly okay again. I'm not sure how that makes me feel."

He looked down at her in surprise and a long silence followed before he answered. "I'll admit the thought of you with him...with anyone if I'm going to be honest, doesn't sit right with me, but I know, better than you can understand, there are times when you're placed in situations and you need to do things you would never have done under normal circumstances."

God did he know that feeling. He gave a small inward shudder and blocked out images of his own he couldn't afford to let loose. He'd been in some of the world's worst hellholes known to mankind, and he knew that in order to survive, people would do anything.

Tully snatched her gaze from his and searched the horizon. "We both have so much happening right now...I'll be going back to Melbourne."

"Who said you have to go back?"

Tully considered his question. The thought had crossed her mind throughout the last few days. "I love my job. I don't think I'm ready to give that up just yet," she said, dropping her eyes to his now covered chest.

Both seemed lost in thought as they mulled over countless possibilities, but in the end there was still so much left that Tully wanted to accomplish in her career. She wasn't ready to throw away the years she'd put into her job and the sacrifices she'd already made to get this far.

"You seem to be putting an awful lot of energy into a job that can't even protect you when you need it the most."

"Jake." Tully sighed, feeling drained. "You don't even have a job. What are you going to do with the rest of your life? How can you make plans about us when you don't even know where you're headed?"

Jake stepped closer, tilting her face up to meet his gaze. "I think you should know I don't give up so easy." He kissed her softly, barely a graze against her lips with his own, to leave her staring after him, her mouth still tingling.

* * * *

That afternoon Jake pulled the rusty old Ute up out the back and told her he wanted to show her something.

They drove along a dirt road, not unlike the driveway they came in on, only heading in the opposite direction. It quickly deteriorated into a rough track, barely distinguishable from the surrounding paddock of spinifex and open grassy scrubland.

The four-wheel drive bounced and jolted along the track and after a while, the open plains gave way to rocky outcrops and a few large gorges carved their path through the barren land. Small pockets of vegetation thickened and followed the rocky ridge.

Tully craned her neck as they emerged upon a small oasis.

It was breathtaking. Out of the vast emptiness came a water hole, surrounded by abundant flora and smooth red and terra-cotta-colored rocks.

"What do you think?" Jake asked, watching the delighted smile spread across her face.

"It's amazing. I can't believe you waited this long to bring me here. I've been sweating my backside off for days."

"Well, you're here now, Chambers, so make the most of it." He shrugged, opening his door without waiting to see if she followed.

He needn't have worried on that score. Tully was close on his heels, nimbly crossing the rocks, eager to feel cool water against her skin.

"Damn," Tully said, coming to a halt at the water's edge. She didn't have any swimmers.

Jake threw her a quick glance, assessing the situation immediately. A grin creased his face, softening the two days' growth of stubble into a disturbingly sexy smirk. "Don't worry, Tully, I promise I won't look if you wanna get naked."

Tully narrowed her eyes dangerously. "You planned this!"

Feigning shocked innocence, he spread his hands wide. "Would I do something like that?"

"Never," she muttered, but stepped out of her shorts and T-shirt, leaving her underwear on, then edged her way into the water. A sigh of pure, unadulterated pleasure escaped her lips and she closed her eyes and floated onto her back.

Bumping into something, Tully opened her eyes and her breath caught as Jake's wet head appeared soundlessly beside her shoulder. He trod water easily beside her and watched with lazy, smoldering eyes.

Mesmerized by the tiny droplets of water beading on his eyelashes, Tully stared like a kangaroo caught in headlights, his hypnotic gaze holding her own hostage. Goose bumps prickled along her arms and a shiver that had nothing to do with cold and everything to do with longing ran through her.

Tully bit her lip, tasting the strange tangy flavor of the water hole. She caught him watching her reaction and realized with a small smirk he wasn't as composed as he had first appeared to be.

She dropped her feet and slipped her arms around his broad neck, allowing him to support both of them in the water. Pulling herself up until she could reach his lips, she pressed her own against them, hungrily savoring the salty, purely Jake taste of his mouth.

He was like a drug, or worse, mud cake. Once you had a taste of him he was downright addictive. She felt him guide them back to the bank of the water hole and her feet touched the rocky bottom of the shallows. They stood, bodies pressed tightly against each other, greedily devouring each other. Tully found it hard to feel where one body stopped and the other started.

Jake broke apart from her and looked deep into her eyes. He brushed the wet strands of hair from her face and took her hand, leading her across the hot rocks to the shade of the trees.

Slowly he slid the strap of her bra off one shoulder, feeling her tremble beneath his fingers as he did so. He followed the path of his fingers with his lips and soon Tully's breath was coming out in short, rough gasps.

Lifting his head, he gave her a look that pierced her very soul. "I don't care who you are, Tully, but right here, right now, you're mine," he told her in a raspy, almost hoarse voice that branded her heart as sure as if he'd used a blazing hot iron.

Tully answered him the only way she could. She stepped out of her remaining clothing and pulled him down onto the ground beside her, showing him with her body what she wasn't sure she could ever promise him.

Especially not with a future that loomed so uncertainly before them.

* * * *

Lying on the warm rocks, their bodies sated and drying after an invigorating swim, Jake broke the gentle silence.

"Would you like to hear how I got hurt?"

"Only if you want to tell me."

He was silent for a long moment, quite possibly facing the demon of sharing a story that few others had heard or would understand. Tully knew how that went.

Finally, he sat up beside her. "We were out on a patrol with the navy." He spoke quietly. "Every now and again we work with them when we're needed. We'd just intercepted some arms and ammunition and other supplies heading for the Taliban, and were returning to the ship when we looked up and saw a smoke trail from shore heading right for us.

He looked into her eyes. "It's the last thing you wanna see, let me tell ya."

He clenched a fist open and shut on his knee in silence before continuing softly. "We hardly had time to brace ourselves and we were hit by an RPG. It tore straight through our boat. The fuel from the boat leaked out into the water and caught on fire, and we had to get rid of all our ops gear. That stuff weighs a ton," he explained with a shake of his head.

Tully may not have had a rocket-propelled grenade launched at her, but she'd had her own experience with riot gear and the protection it offered. She could only imagine how vulnerable he'd have been in a war zone without his protective gear.

"You stood no chance in the water with it all on."

He stared out at the water for a moment, then, as if he hadn't heard her, went on. "There were bodies everywhere, people on fire. I could hear one of my men calling from up in the wheelhouse—his leg was shattered in the explosion. The boat was sinking fast, so I had to smash through the front window. I climbed in to help him, but the roof fell in, knocking me down. The whole place on fire—I could feel it burning into me." He turned his head away from her slightly, bent to pick up a stone, and skipped it across the water. Water she now wondered if he even saw. He seemed to be somewhere far, far away.

She sat up beside him, placed a palm on his shoulder. "Jake... you don't have to..."

He held up a hand, stopping her attempt to comfort him. "No. Let me finish. I need to get this out of me. Without any gear on there was nothing to protect me from the fire. I managed to shield my head but my chest and back caught the brunt of it. Somehow I got out and dragged my mate out of the cabin. By this time the boat was almost under, literally sinking beneath our feet." He paused, his fist clenching and unclenching as he relived the memories.

"Have you ever seen burning water?" He glanced over at her and she shook her head mutely, even though she was sure it was a rhetorical question.

"I remember looking all around us, seeing the water was on fire. Thinking how weird that sounded, how it should be impossible. Sometimes I can still smell it, the smell of death. Everything burning." He paused, looking down at the ground but no doubt seeing images of that horrible day flashing before his eyes. Tully knew about flashbacks.

"I dived under the water and all I could see was floating debris and lifeless bodies. Above me the water was alight and I was trying to hold my breath but knew I had to come up for air eventually."

Tully hadn't realized she had been holding her own breath as she listened to his story. She reached out and took his hand in hers.

"I remember breaking through to the surface and seeing a rescue boat coming toward us. I think I was more worried at that point about passing out. I knew if I did I probably wouldn't make it. I remember the look on the face of the MO and thinking 'it must be bad if he looks that worried.'"

He gave her hand a gentle squeeze and released it, leaving Tully feeling oddly bereft. "I was in and out of consciousness over the next few hours and don't really remember much until I was stable in a military hospital in Germany."

He sighed and moved to lie on his back again beside her. Tully stayed where she was and peered down at him. "I'm sorry about your friends. I guess we have that in common, we've both lost friends through senseless acts of violence," she said quietly.

He reached for her hand, and looked into her eyes. "We'll make it through this, Tully," he promised.

Before she could answer, Jake pulled her back down to meet his lips and she was lost in the smell of sun-kissed skin and the feel of his strong hands and lips caressing her body—strong, capable hands and lips that drove the nightmares they had both lived through far, far away...

Replacing them with hope.

* * * *

That evening, under a magnificent red, blue, and orange sunset, they made a fire and sat side by side. All around them, the ancient landscape darkened, transforming into mystical-like silhouettes. Trees, black against a palate of spectacular color in the never-ending sky, made the perfect backdrop as the fire crackled and popped cozily. In its glow Tully felt as though anything were possible.

Lying in Jake's embrace, she felt his heartbeat, steady and reassuring beneath her ear. The stars shimmered over their heads like a billion shining diamonds scattered carelessly across the heavens. She savored everything, storing the sights, sounds, and smells in her memory, reluctant to acknowledge the insistent niggling which whispered a warning that trouble was coming.

It seemed to permeate the very air around her, and if the small frown that marred his brow was anything to go by when he thought she wasn't watching him, she suspected Jake sensed it as well.

Turning in his embrace, she pushed the sound of ticking as far as she could to the back of her mind and let Jake sweep her away to a place where there was no lurking danger and they were safe.

Chapter Thirteen

The air was cool and as Tully opened her eyes she saw the lightening of the sky as the sun slowly made its appearance. A blurry form paced a few feet away from her, talking in a low, calm voice into his phone.

Sitting up, Tully stretched out the kinks and groaned. No matter how romantic the idea seemed at the time she was not going to sleep under the stars again. It was stupid to subject the human body to hard ground and the elements all night.

Jake walked back toward her and leaned down to hold out a hand.

"You did this for a living?" She felt sore and grumpy as he pulled her upright.

"Not unless I had to. I prefer a bed any day." He sent her a wink and a grin but it was soon replaced with a look that Tully was beginning to recognize.

She noticed he'd been up and already dressed.

"Are we going somewhere?"

He flicked a brief glance in her direction as he squatted by the fire, tipping a can of water over the remains to make sure it was out. "I'm going out to check on a few things."

"What things?"

"I've had a couple of...contingency plans in place. Just going to check they're all intact." He held up his hand in warning when her interest piqued. "It's better you don't know...you being a cop and all."

"You're right. I don't want to know. I need a coffee." She paused as she passed him on her way to the Ute, circling her arms around his waist, needing to feel the comfort of his body against her own. Wrapped in a tight embrace, there were no words, just the steady thumping of two hearts and, for one fleeting moment in time, she felt safe.

* * * *

Once home, Tully took a quick shower and found some clean clothes. As she came back into the kitchen and poured a coffee, she eyed Jake standing with his arms braced against the back of a kitchen chair, a serious expression on his handsome face.

"Tully, I need you to be prepared just in case anything goes wrong, okay? You know where the guns and the ammo are, right?" he asked, then continued when she nodded. "If I call and tell you to get out I want you to take the Ute in the shed and head west until you reach the water hole. Okay? Someone will find you. Don't go back toward the road." He sent her a lopsided grin. "I've planted a few surprises under the cattle grids and along the road in case we get unexpected guests." He squeezed her hand and his expression softened. "It's going to be all right. I just want you to know there's a backup plan. Okay?"

He smiled to reassure her and she felt like crying. She nodded and tried to smile back.

"Tully, when I get back I want to talk to you about something. I've been thinking about our dilemma and I might have a solution. Promise me you won't make up your mind about us until I get back, okay?"

Great. Way to keep a woman in suspense. Leave with a bombshell like that hanging over my head.

"I'll wait until you get back," she agreed.

Jake kissed her briefly, and then disappeared out the back door. She watched his car drive away, leaving a trail of dust in his wake, until she couldn't see him anymore.

For a moment she allowed herself the luxury of release. She was wound tighter than a bareback rider's hand in a rope. If this situation turned bad she would need a clear head. From previous experience she knew the tears she gave in to now were a side effect of stress and once she released that stress she would be free to concentrate on the job at hand.

Well, that was the theory anyway. As she buried her head in her hands now, though, she wondered if maybe this time she'd bitten off more than she could chew.

* * * *

The isolation had become more than a little daunting, and for a few minutes Tully battled a rising panic that seemed to come from nowhere. Chiding herself for being melodramatic, she reasoned out her fear, realizing it came from feeling so tiny against the immense endless miles around her.

Thinking back to the day before, she tried to focus on the

beauty of the place and not the isolation of it. This worked for a while until a strange pining for Jake replaced her panic and she had to remind herself of the dangers of acting like a lovesick teenager, instead of a capable, strong woman. When she finally felt as though she had her fears and mindset back under control she was able to focus once more.

Mid-morning she went out into the shed to poke around and familiarize herself with the Ute, as she recalled Jake's warning. Like Jake, she also liked to be prepared and soon her professionalism took over and she began to run scenarios through her head until she was certain she was ready in the event of Jake's phone call. She dug her spare gun out of her tote bag and placed it in the Ute, just in case. It would help to have an extra she was familiar with close by.

A strange droning noise seemed to be hovering in the distance. She looked up and scanned the driveway but saw no telltale billow of dirt or speck in the distance. The noise, though, seemed to get closer, and by the time her brain registered the sound, the helicopter high in the sky had begun its rapid descent.

A trickle of apprehension raced up her spine as she watched, squinting against the vivid blue sky, the speck grow larger. She had no idea why a chopper would be coming here, unless it had something to do with the case. There could be a legitimate reason behind the visit. With the exception of Jake and their lovemaking, however, life had taught her to be cautious. She wasn't about to take any chances now.

She wondered if Jake had heard it and if he were on his way back. She hoped he wasn't too far away.

Removing her Glock, which Jake had considerately managed to bring along as well, she slipped a spare clip into her pocket from the backpack in the Ute as a precaution. She made her way to the doorway of the machinery shed to find a clear vantage point where she could observe the occupants of the helicopter before she went out to greet them.

The chopper made a slow descent to the clearing between the shed and the homestead, and Tully lost it in the swirl of dust and debris that the rotor blades stirred up as it touched down gently. The door opened and a figure stepped out. At once Tully's breath escaped in a small sigh of relief.

Louise Bollinger's slim figure climbed from the aircraft. She looked back inside the chopper at another occupant Tully couldn't see from her position and, after receiving some kind of instruction, headed toward the house and opened the squeaky yard gate.

Something held Tully back from showing herself. She hadn't given Louise her location, so how did her boss know where to find her? Staying in the shed, Tully kept her eye on the helicopter and the occupants inside, waiting for Louise to reappear once she established no one was home. She didn't have long to wait, and Tully knew she had been right in waiting before she announced herself.

In her hand Louise had a gun and, as she scanned the area, Tully saw she was not happy.

"There's no one here," Louise called from the gate as she headed back toward the chopper. The door opened again and another figure finally stepped out.

Tully felt perspiration slide down her back and went cold. Louise's companion was Leonardo Spiros, someone her boss should not be sharing a helicopter with under any stretch of the imagination.

"We need to search the area. Call in the men. We can't cover an area this big alone. She can't be far," Louise told an impeccably dressed Leonardo, who stood looking about him with a snarl of disgust on his face.

"Make the call, but do it fast. I don't want to be here any longer than I have to be," he told Louise as she came to a stop before him and punched in a number on her mobile, already turning away from him to speak into the phone abruptly.

Tully pulled further back into the shadows and tried to remain calm. They would have backup arriving and, once they did, every inch of this place would be searched, including this shed. She would have no hope of remaining hidden then.

Think. Where would she go? On foot she would at least be able to slip away undetected...maybe, but she wouldn't stand a chance out there. With little vegetation to hide her, men in vehicles would catch up with her in no time. Her gaze came to rest on the Ute. It would also be useless. They'd hear her straightaway and, although it was faster than on foot, it was hardly built for speed. Even with a head start they would catch up with her.

Tully went over her options. There was a pilot plus Louise and Leonardo. If she were to have any chance at all she would have to take them down here, alone, right now, before their backup arrived.

She knew Louise was armed. There was little doubt Leonardo would also have a weapon. If the pilot was a Spiros employee he might also have a gun. Three against one...not great odds but better than the odds due to arrive by road any minute.

Taking out her Glock, Tully crouched and circled around the back of the shed so she could come at them from the rear of the chopper. The pilot was taking the opportunity to have a smoke. He sat on his haunches, looking out over the vast expanse of brown paddock, savoring his tobacco. Tully gave a sharp smack with the butt of her gun to the side of his head, dropping him like a sack of potatoes. Grabbing his shoulders, she managed to drag him behind the corner of the shed. He wouldn't be very well hidden if someone came around to look for him, but he was out of the way for now.

Stepping over the prone pilot, she crouched low and crept toward the helicopter. The radio was crackling with conversation and it crossed her mind to use it to get help, but she couldn't get to it without alerting Leonardo, who stood with his arms braced against the rail, looking at the house before him with utter contempt.

Tully moved behind him until she was close enough to put her gun to his head but as she went to do just that, she heard, "Don't do anything stupid."

Tully flinched in surprise as her boss's once familiar voice sounded coldly from behind her. Slowly Leonardo turned to face her and Tully saw a glimmer of something bitter and dangerous shimmer in the depths of his hard gaze. Tully watched, helpless, as her gun was removed and she was left without a weapon to defend herself. Cursing her own stupidity for allowing her defenses to be so low that she'd forgone her usual rule of always carrying her backup weapon—she found herself standing before a man who had vowed to exact his revenge on her all those many months ago.

"I've been waiting a long time to see you again. I'm sorry I'm a little bit confused as to what your name is." Leonardo's dark eyes slithered across her body, making Tully's skin crawl.

Tully watched as he circled her, gritting her teeth when he stepped close behind her and spoke softly into her ear.

"Imagine my surprise when I was told the woman I knew as Georgia Preston was in fact Detective Georgia Tully."

Tully jerked her head away from his lips, her skin crawling. "Imagine my surprise when I found out you weren't in prison yet."

She saw a smug look cross his face. "You don't seriously think that's going to happen, do you, Georgia?" he chastised with a mocking tsk-tsk sound.

Tully didn't bother to answer. She turned her attention instead to the woman who stood before her.

"Him, I get," Tully said dismissively with a slight nod of her head toward Leonardo, "but I don't have a clue what your place is in all of this." Her voice could not disguise the betrayal she was trying to come to terms with.

Louise gave a bitter tinkle of a laugh. "You really put your foot in it this time, didn't you? Surely even you, little Miss Dudley Do-Right, had to have thought twice about messing with some-one like the Spiros family," Louise said, ignoring Tully's question completely.

"I don't understand, Louise. What on earth could you possibly be thinking?"

"She wasn't, were you, Louise?" Leo put in with a snigger. "Love does that to a person, makes them forget common sense and risk everything. Have you ever felt that, Georgia?"

Tully frowned as she digested the news. Louise in love? How had she missed the signs? Maybe Louise had been too good an actress and able to hide emotions most people couldn't.

"Shut up, Leo," Louise snarled, shooting him a stare that stopped his ranting.

"In love with whom?" Tully asked, more than a little confused, until a thought crossed her mind. "Not you and Leo?"

Under normal circumstances Louise's look of abstract horror would have been entertaining. It seemed a lot less funny somehow when she held a gun.

"My father, of course. Don't tell me the mighty Detective Tully didn't figure it out," Leo scoffed.

Tully stared at them in disbelief. Her boss was having an affair with the police force's most wanted man? Louise's own colleagues, fellow officers of the law, had been murdered by this man, and she was in love with him?

"You know what Spiros has done. You know what he's involved in. You're supposed to be upholding the law!"

"Oh, don't look so shocked, Georgia," Louise snapped. "Your silly little notion that good will always be rewarded and evil pun-ished is an immature childhood fantasy. There's no reward for sit-ting quietly on the sidelines. If you want something in this world then you have to take it, because if you wait politely someone else will just step on you."

Tully wondered if she had fallen into some kind of weird alter-nate universe and this was her boss's evil twin sister.

Behind them, inside the helicopter, the radio sprang to life, an anxious voice calling in that they had come under fire. Louise crossed to grab the hand piece. "What's happening, Dimitri?" she demanded without taking her attention from Tully.

Static sounded loud in the small cockpit and Dimitri could be heard yelling over the distinctive background sound of gunfire before the communications went dead. No amount of calling summoned a response and Louise threw down the radio with a growl.

"Get inside the house, Georgia," she ordered, giving Tully a push to get her moving.

Walking into the house, Tully began to reassess her situation. There were two of them, both had a weapon, but their entourage seemed to be delayed. This was a bonus. There were more guns in the shed as well as the Ute so she had both weapons and transportation nearby.

Okay, this situation isn't totally unsalvageable, she thought with renewed optimism just as a blow caught her across the back of the head.

Chapter Fourteen

Tully stifled a moan of pain. Her head throbbed. She tried to open her eyes but that took far too much effort. She decided to wait until the insistent throbbing came to a stop. She had no idea how long she'd been out for, but one thing was certain, she was so over the whole getting-hit-over-the-head thing. Enough was enough.

As things began to clear, Tully became aware of voices raised in dispute.

"I'm not finished with her yet," Leonardo said coldly.

"We don't have time to mess around. Need I remind you this cannot lead back to you or your father at this point in time?" Louise's clipped, condescending tone was followed by the brusque clip-clop of her heels on timber flooring.

Tully investigated the extent of her injuries. Her hands were tied behind her back. She wiggled her fingers, relieved to find they were all in working order. She had been dumped on her side, the smell of old timber strong in her nose and, under her cheek, she could feel the rough texture of the wooden floor. From the other smells she figured she was inside the farmhouse and hope flared inside her. At least she hadn't left the area and Jake might still find her. She risked a peek and blinked as her blurred vision cleared and she was able to see where she was.

The arguing continued and Tully was able to pin their position to somewhere in the kitchen area, judging from the distance to where she lay in the living room.

"Louise, you may have my father on a tight leash, but need I remind you he might soon be, rather unfortunately, out of the picture, locked up in prison for a very long time? What will you do then I wonder?"

"Threats, Leonardo? Do you think that's a wise move? I've had to risk my entire career and reputation to come out here and clean up your mess. Do *not* make the mistake of thinking I'm going to quietly hand over the reins of this business to you if your father goes down. I have too much invested in this to walk away."

"You are no more than my father's mistress. You honestly think you're going to be able to walk in and take over my family's business?"

"I think you and I both know I am much more than your father's mistress. Without me the family won't have any protection from the police."

"How lucky that you are there to protect us. You've done such a wonderful job so far. Father's in jail, both sons under investigation. With friends like you, Inspector Bollinger, who needs enemies?"

"Who brought an undercover detective into the family?" she taunted.

Tully scanned the room and weighed her options. While they were fighting amongst themselves, they were leaving her alone. Tugging on her ropes behind her back, she soon realized getting out of here wasn't going to be as easy as she'd first thought. Rolling onto her back, she winced as her arms strained behind her, but forced herself into a sitting position with her back against the wall.

Her head pounded in a headache to end all headaches, but she forced a determination into her tired body she hadn't thought she possessed. She had to escape. It couldn't end like this. Not after everything she had been through.

Think, Tully. What would Jake do? She caught a rogue sob and blinked back tears. *Get a grip.* Angrily she pushed away the fear, fighting for control. She wasn't going to get anywhere if she started crying.

Pushing back against the wall, she slid herself upright using the wall as support, and then tiptoed across the floor to the window. Turning her back, she fumbled with the latch on the window and tried to push it up, unsure if there would be any noise to give her away or not. As it turned out she didn't have a hope of budging the stupid thing. The elements and age had made sure there was no chance of it sliding open in order for her to climb through, not without the use of a jackhammer and both hands anyway.

There were two other choices—the kitchen, which at the moment held the two people she was trying to evade, pretty much ruling that option out, or the front door that was located at the opposite end of the hallway. The risk with that alternative was, of course, being seen from the kitchen, making it only somewhat less dangerous than the other.

Making her way in a cautious, crab-like movement, she edged her way up the hallway, never before noticing just how long the damn thing was until now.

At long last the end came into sight. The screen door, however, would be a problem. She knew it squeaked.

Keeping her focus on the opposite end of the hall, she eased herself back against the screen, praying with each passing second the noise would be minimal enough to be ignored. Her hands still tied behind her, she pushed gently against the stiff, old-fashioned flyscreen beneath her fingers.

Finally the gap was wide enough for her to slide through. Her heart gave a small leap of excitement. *Almost there*. She winced as the tired old door creaked a protest.

Leo's mocking announcement sent chills up her spine from the veranda behind her. "I almost feel bad letting you think you'd gotten this far...almost."

Damn, Tully thought in dismay. *He must have circled around from outside*. Twisting and tugging on her bindings, it could have been a trick of her desperate mind, but she was sure they were beginning to loosen. If she could keep him talking and distracted long enough, she might have a chance to get out of the ropes.

"Look, Leo, it wasn't personal, you know. It was just unfortunate you and your family are a bunch of low-life criminals. I was just doing my job."

The bitterness in his eyes and the twist of his mouth were a sure sign her comments had struck a nerve. Her mind was already fleeing to another serious matter. Where the hell was Louise? Did Leo have a gun?

"Louise left me to tie up loose ends. She was pushing for a more immediate end but I wanted to see you one last time, to make you hurt the way I did," he told her, with a voice that sounded childishly gleeful.

As she inched little by little along the veranda, he stalked her with the calmness of a cat toying with a mouse.

"I'm glad there were no hard feelings, then," she murmured. The ropes were definitely looser, but she still needed more time. Her wrists burnt with the friction of rope rubbing against skin but she ignored the pain, her only desire to get away from this lunatic in one piece and find Jake. "Are you sure Louise said you should do this?"

"Louise doesn't give me orders. I'm the head of the Spiros family now, or hadn't you heard?" he asked her bitterly.

"How long do you think Louise and your father will let you think that for? People are going to suspect you had something to do with the disappearance of an undercover detective on your own case." Tully shook her head and gave him her best pitying expression.

His eyes flared and Tully winced. She needed to provoke his anger and outrage if she was going to get out of this, but it was hard to go against every ounce of self-preservation she possessed to deliberately piss off an unstable madman.

"Louise and your father, together, that's a pretty tough act to follow. You think you're up to taking over from them? Face it, Leo, you're not the brightest bulb in the packet. I mean, think about it, who's your father going to trust his empire with? The woman he loves and admires, or his son, who pretty much single-hand-edly destroyed the family?" Her hands continued to work behind her back. "I suppose they'll need you to look like you're running things, particularly if she's hoping to keep her day job." Tully dropped her voice sarcastically. "Some people could consider it a conflict of interest if she tries to do both."

A mask of hatred seemed frozen on Leo's face and she was running out of room to back away from him.

"I can understand how you'd feel put out—flesh and blood and only used as a front, while Louise and your father run things from afar," Tully continued, watching his every move like a hawk.

"My *family*," he stressed in quiet rage, "is none of your concern, Detective."

She just needed to push him that little bit further. "I'm sorry, Leo, you know about the whole letting-you-believe-I-loved-you thing." She shrugged. "The guys wanted to find an angle and they saw you as the weakest link. It was actually pretty brilliant when you think about it...play on the underachiever." She paused before adding, "Build him up a bit, make him feel like he had a backbone for a change. You were very pliable, Leo. Your dad did a wonderful job screwing you up."

There it was, the flash she had been waiting for. Even though she braced herself for the blow that knocked her flying backward against the wall, it momentarily dazed her, and she fought to keep her wits about her. From the corner of her eye she'd seen the small tomahawk-like axe Jake had used for splitting kindling for their campfire, on top of the woodpile.

As Leo ran at her, she managed to kick him hard in the face, which sent him sprawling backward and gave her time to scavenge for the axe behind her with her still-bound hands, grateful the rope had loosened enough to allow her a workable amount of maneuverability.

She kept her eyes fastened upon Leo as he shook his head to clear his vision and came at her once more. "You know, I remember your partner. Spencer, wasn't it?"

Tully filled with sharp loathing, and she saw the triumph light up in Leo's eyes. "I remember he begged." He gave a chilling snigger. "Please, don't do it," he taunted in a whimpering tone.

She had to wait until he was close enough. He lashed out but she kicked hard at his groin, and dropped him to his knees with a soundless scream of pain etched upon his crazed face.

She juggled the axe she still clutched firmly in her hands, feeling the cold, sharp blade between her wrists. Feverishly she worked the blade against the rope until she felt something snap. The rope was so old it hadn't needed much encouragement for the twines to all but disintegrate and she could finally pull free of her restraints.

She kicked Leonardo's feet out from beneath him as he struggled to a standing position once more, fury and hatred driving him on. Still holding his groin and struggling to catch his breath, he ignored her warning to stay down.

Falling back on her training, she had him restrained without much protest. A well-placed knee to his already tender groin was not technically called for at that point but made her feel better, rendering him practically inert.

Bending down close to his ear she whispered, "That one was for Spence, you coward," before she shoved the shirt she'd been wearing over her undershirt into his mouth to keep him quiet. Securing his hands with her belt, Tully then dropped her head and took a deep breath.

Chapter Fifteen

Now that the immediate danger had passed, Tully registered her hands were beginning to throb. Cradling her sore wrists against the front of her body she saw they were covered in blood. In her hurry to cut through the rope earlier, she'd also cut herself. A steady river of blood flowed freely down her arm.

She dropped her attention to her captive, ripped at his silk shirt, and wrapped her wound in the fabric to stem the blood loss. It wasn't ideal but it would have to do for now. Before she could relax, she would need to locate Louise.

Leaning over Leo's incensed form, she searched his body for a weapon, eventually finding one in the waistband of his tailored trousers. She stepped over him and made her way around the house to where the chopper waited. As she surveyed the area, she noted the groggy pilot sat, head braced in his hands, in the front seat, while an impatient Louise paced back and forth, anxiously searching the horizon for something.

Maybe she'd heard from the reinforcements and they were on their way. It wouldn't leave much time to get away from here if that were the case. Tully made a brief detour inside the house to gather a few supplies.

She searched for her mobile, cursing when she couldn't find it. A glance out the window toward the chopper made her heart lurch. Louise was no longer there.

"Damn it," Tully muttered beneath her breath. She'd probably gotten tired of Leo taking so long and gone looking for him. Crouching low, Tully pushed open the kitchen door and eased out, being as quiet as she could. Leo was around the other side of the house and she made her way through the overgrown garden to circle around.

Louise was crouched over his body about to remove the gag from his mouth when she suddenly sensed Tully's presence and glanced up, drawing her weapon at the same time.

"Put it down, Louise. It's over."

Louise gave a somewhat amused chuckle, but it didn't reach her eyes. Those remained hard and empty of anything except the desire to win. "There's a small army of men on their way here,

Georgia. You may think you have it all under control, but there's no way you're going to be able to hold all of us off. You throw your gun down and I'll do my best to protect you," she offered with malicious delight.

"I don't think you should be too sure about the cavalry arriving."

"Why? You think your little bodyguard has taken care of them? I think you'll find he might be the obstacle they just radioed in to tell me they had eliminated and were bringing back, but I guess we can wait and see."

In the distance Tully could see a plume of dust rising along the road leading toward the farmhouse. The thumping of her heart became painful. Surely Louise was bluffing about Jake, and yet she was telling the truth about the men on their way. The vehicle was getting larger by the minute.

Panic threatened to surface but she forced herself to remain calm. *The worst thing you can do in a situation like this is to panic. Take a breath. Now think. What are your options?*

The chopper sat nearby and that was her first instinct. Get Louise into the chopper and out of here, but then there was Leo, and he was the one she wanted even more. Did she have enough time to drag him into the chopper as well as secure Louise? Her gut told her no. Louise wasn't going to give up without a fight. She had too much to lose. She wouldn't be making it easy, stalling for time in order to allow her backup to get here.

The house? Maybe she could get them inside the house and hold them off, yet there was only one of her and too many of them to hold off in an unsecured house alone. Damn it.

She considered the Ute, but she still wouldn't be able to outrun the larger four-wheel drive and to be caught out there in the middle of nowhere would be disastrous.

The sun was burning her shoulders and sweat trickled down her back and between her breasts as she stood there, a gun on her boss and a bunch of thugs on their way to kill her. It was times like this she wished she'd been just a bartender from Townsville for real.

Making the decision, she ducked to one side, catching Louise unaware, still holding Tully in her sights. As she threw herself to the side, she fired her gun and Louise ducked and took cover. Running toward the shed where the Ute was stored, Tully made her choice. She would stand her ground from the shed. It only had one opening, three secure sides, and, more important, a Ute with weapons and ammunition.

She no longer had her two prisoners, but there wasn't much she could do about that now. If Louise wasn't bluffing, then Jake might not be around to help out and Tully would be fighting to save her life.

Louise yelled from outside to come out, but wasn't too keen on showing herself, unsure exactly where Tully had disappeared to.

She was taking the cautious route, waiting for backup, before she got too brave.

From her position Tully could see the vehicle take shape. It would be there in just a few minutes, its big black presence like an apparition from hell. Dust spewed from its rear like a vicious scorpion's tail lashing and swirling angrily behind it.

She dug out the guns from the Ute and loaded them, placing them within easy reach for when she would need them.

The four-wheel drive approached the cattle grid and didn't bother slowing down. Hidden within the dust screen a door flew open and something fell from the vehicle, but nobody outside saw it. Then, in an ear-splintering blast, the big car was thrown across the red dirt like a child's unwanted toy, rolling and smashing across the rough terrain. The cattle grid and fence posts were alight and thick black smoke poured from the wrecked body of the vehicle.

Shock was soon replaced by instinct and training. Tully didn't have time to stand around and work out what had happened. She had a fair idea one of Jake's little surprises had just been discovered. Had he been a prisoner in the vehicle? Was he safe? The thoughts rushed through her mind and as quickly as they formed she shoved them away. Not now. She couldn't think about Jake, couldn't go there without losing her edge. If he were out there, injured, he would need her to focus and get out of this in order to help him.

Grabbing an extra rifle she crouched low and ran from the shed toward the last place she'd heard Louise yelling from.

Louise was staring at the catastrophe across the paddock and slow to turn as Tully snuck up behind her.

"Put down the gun and get to your knees, Louise."

Tully helped her along with a none-too-gentle shove, dropped a set of handcuffs into her boss's lap, and told her to put them on. She gripped the woman's wrists and squeezed the cuffs until she was satisfied they were firm enough to hold.

Tully's gaze lifted to focus on the crackling inferno that had engulfed the once-gleaming four-wheel drive.

Ideally she would like to have gone over to search for survivors, but she didn't have the manpower. She prayed no one had survived, criminal or not. No one deserved to suffer the kind of injuries any survivor from that would have sustained.

"Was revenge for Spencer really worth all this carnage, Georgia?" The harsh words came from the woman in cuffs beside her.

For the briefest of moments a picture of Spence flashed before Tully's eyes and her hand trembled. This abhorrent betrayal by the woman she'd once looked up to almost pushed her to do more than disarm and arrest her, but belief in her job, despite Louise poking fun at her morals, was the one thing that separated the two women. Tully could never cross that very distinct line between right and wrong.

A small, ironic grin broke out across her face as she looked at the woman spluttering obscenities at her. "I bet I'm living out a lot of people's fantasies right now, having their boss grovelling at their feet. Get up, Louise." She dragged the woman to her feet. The whine of rotor blades starting up snapped her attention toward the helicopter. The pilot sat in his seat, pale and looking far from happy.

With a shove Tully hurried Louise toward the chopper and the now frantic pilot who was calling for help into the mic of his radio. "Oh my God, she's coming, she's got a gun..."

"Oh, for God's sake get off that radio and don't you even think about taking off without us. I'm not going to hurt you." When he eyed her doubtfully she added, "I'm a police officer. It's okay."

The pilot looked from one woman to the other. "That's what she said too. How do I know you're really a cop?" he challenged with a belligerent tone.

"What's your name?" Tully demanded.

"Mike."

"Well, Mike, considering I'm holding the gun I'd just go with the theory that I'm the one telling the truth. Are you up to flying?" she asked, as she eyed his pale face.

"Do I have a choice?"

"Do I look like I'm in the mood to argue with you?"

He considered it for a fraction of a second, then nodded his head, wincing as he did so. "I can fly."

"Will this thing carry three passengers as far as Darwin?" She eyed the metallic blue and white helicopter.

"Lady, this is a Robinson R44. It'll do 200 kilometers an hour. It has about three and a half hours flight time, max."

"I don't want to buy the damn thing," she broke in impatiently. "I only need to know how far you can take us."

"It's got just under half a tank left. There's no way this thing will carry the weight of three passengers and a pilot as far as Darwin."

"I need to go and find the other one, and then I need you to fly us out of here to the nearest police station. Okay?"

The pilot gave a small nod, mindful of his tender head this time.

Tully felt woozy and a cold sweat covered her body despite the unrelenting heat of the day. Her wound was bleeding, soaking through the makeshift bandage and she was facing the very real risk of passing out if she didn't sit down soon. There was no time to worry about it. She had to get out of this place and find help.

She came to a stop as she rounded the corner. The veranda was empty.

Somehow, during all the mayhem, Leo had managed to get away. Was nothing going to be easy today?

About to turn, she was knocked sideways and landed, hard, on the ground, staring up at an enraged Leo. In his hands he held the axe she'd forgotten to remove in her haste to locate Louise.

He stood panting above her, his arms still bound by the belt, then gave a crazed cry as he raised the axe above his head. Tully saw it happen but in her weakened state was unable to roll out of the way in time. She saw the sharp blade falling toward her and screamed in terror...

The axe seemed to freeze in midair and a peculiar expression crossed Leo's face as he stared down at her in wide-eyed surprise. Tully gaped as a deep, red shadow spread rapidly across the front of his body. He staggered and collapsed into a crumpled heap by her side.

Scrambling away from him, Tully's mind registered that Leo had been shot, but she had no idea by whom or if she were next. She got to her feet and ran for the house. Halfway up the steps she heard her name being called and her steps faltered.

Turning, she saw Jake running to her from across the yard. With a sob of relief, she fell into his strong arms, allowing his warmth and security to shelter her.

She pulled back enough to look up into his concerned eyes. He was covered in dirt and sweat and there was dried blood on his face. Tully had never seen a man she desired more than the one right in front of her.

"Where did you come from?"

A wide smile split his face and her heart did a mad flip. "Caught a lift in that." He threw his thumb in the direction of the wreckage. He took in her pale face and sat her down on the top step. "Let me check you over."

"I'm okay," she told him even though her voice trembled.

"You're not okay. You're hurt, Tully." He inspected her hastily wrapped arm and the amount of blood that had seeped through.

"There's no time to worry about that. I have to get back to Louise, get her into custody. She was working with them," Tully said, still unable to come to terms with the fact the woman she'd admired for so long was a criminal.

"It's okay. I have someone over there with her, and she isn't going anywhere," Jake said, taking her face in his hands and forcing her to look at him in order to assess her state.

Tully pushed at his hands irritably as he ran them over her, searching for any other injuries. "I'm okay," she assured him.

"You'll live," he agreed, "but you have to get out of here. There's another carload of Spiros's men on the way."

Tully met his eyes as conflicting emotions battled within. She needed to get Louise to authorities as soon as possible, and yet Jake was telling her the danger hadn't passed. That he would be staying here to face it and with little help.

"I'm not leaving you out here, Jake. This is my problem."

"Well, I'm making it my problem. You've done your bit. You need to get that woman into custody and let me do what I've been trained to do out here," he told her as he reverted to the unrelenting professional he was in times of danger. "It's okay, Tully. We've managed to even the odds a bit," he said, tossing his head toward the wreckage behind them.

"I don't want to leave you," she told him, her voice husky with emotion. She saw his eyes soften and a smile tugged at his mouth.

"You have no idea how long I've been waiting to hear those words, Chambers, but you need to get out of here, now."

He was right. While they stood here and wasted precious time arguing about it, they could all become targets.

She asked for his phone and quickly pushed in a series of numbers, gave a brief rundown, and placed the phone carefully back in her front pocket. With Jake's assistance they made their way back to the helicopter where a man Tully had never seen before stood over Louise's incensed form. He seemed unaffected by the tirade of obscenities she was yelling at him.

Louise stopped abusing the man at her approach. "You have no idea how much trouble you're in, Georgia."

"I'm pretty sure it's not as much trouble as you're in. Let me make one thing perfectly clear, you are no longer anything more to me than a criminal about to be escorted into custody. Understand?" Tully's voice was cold, devoid of any respect she'd formerly held for her superior.

"You're a fool. You've just signed your death warrant by killing a Spiros. You won't make it to that trial alive."

"Then I've got nothing to lose, have I?"

"What a pity, you're finally showing some spirit," Louise mocked in a cold tone.

"Get in the chopper, Louise," Tully ordered. The man with the gun dragged her to her feet. Tully almost took delight in seeing the flicker of alarm that flashed across the woman's face. She slid into the aircraft sending a look of pure contempt over her shoulder at her former colleague and protégé.

Jake double-checked the cuffs, then turned to help Tully into the chopper. "I'll find you as soon as I can," he promised, then kissed her. As far as kisses went, it was brief, barely a few seconds in time, but in it was a pledge.

Then he was gone, running back toward cover, the two men disappearing from sight like a pair of shadowy apparitions.

Louise's mocking voice cut into Tully's thoughts with the same effect as fingernails down a chalkboard. "There are at least a dozen armed men on their way here. You honestly think your little boyfriend is going to be able to hold them off? Things will go much better for him if you let me go."

Tully turned her attention back to the task at hand, suppressing the panic that threatened at the thought of Jake's life in danger. "You know, I still can't fathom how someone like you could possibly fall for a scumbag like Spiros."

Louise's eyes flashed with resentment before that mad gleam surfaced once again. "I finally found a man who saw the leadership qualities in me the force continued to overlook. We took his family wealth and power and tripled it in just six months. It was perfect until the damn task force decided to target us." A shrill laugh echoed through the cockpit. "Imagine my surprise when I discovered one of my own detectives was the very person designated to bring it all down."

"You had a whole career ahead of you. Why would you throw that away?" Tully asked in bewilderment, shaking her head.

"Why? Because I'm sick of fighting the system. Women will never be equal in the force. When the going gets tough they always go back to the good ole boys club. They treat women like a joke, give us titles and prestige, but laugh at us behind our backs and take away any real power we have." She spat, her eyes glittering with savagery. "Do you have any idea the humiliation I have endured to get to where I am today? I can guarantee no man in the force has ever had to sacrifice the way I have."

Tully looked at her former boss and shook her head in amazement. She'd heard this all before of course. Louise had constantly spouted discrimination theories but had Tully realized just how personal the woman had been taking it, she might have noticed the extent of that hatred and jealousy that simmered beneath the surface.

"It's just a shame the one man you *don't* despise happens to be a criminal who turned you into one too. Still, I guess you'll have a lot more in common with him now, since you'll both be in prison," Tully said grimly.

"You're assuming, Georgia, that my career is over. What makes you think you're actually going to get away with any of this? I'm a superintendent and you're holding me at gunpoint," she pointed out calmly. "It will be your word against mine."

Tully gave a small smile but didn't reply, switching her attention to the pilot. "How long will it take to reach the nearest town?"

"About twenty minutes to Ginndawandi, but the police station isn't manned all the time," he warned.

"Then where's the next biggest town?" Tully asked, trying to keep the frustration from her voice.

"It will be a stretch but I think we can make it as far as Katherine."

Tully nodded and slammed the door shut, giving her prisoner one last look to make sure she was secure.

The roar of the engine was deafening. Dust billowed around them as they slowly rose from the ground and hovered above the old farmhouse before turning to face the east and gathering speed. Red dirt and scrubby trees grew smaller, until eventually they resembled nothing more than part of a crazy patchwork quilt below them. In the distance the telltale plume of dust announced the arrival of unwelcome guests. Anxiously, Tully searched the landscape below for Jake and his men, but there was no sign of them. He was well trained and knew his surroundings. He had the advantage of both skill and battle experience. Spiros's men, on the other hand, would be little more than hired thugs with little experience outside the city. Still, as the helicopter banked and pulled away from the house leaving him down there to face them without her, Tully felt torn.

Tully had the pilot radio the control tower to have police on-site when they arrived and to send out some reinforcements to the property immediately, but she knew that by the time help arrived for Jake and the others, it would be all over, one way or the other.

Chapter Sixteen

The moment the helicopter touched down it was surrounded by armed police and enough security to disarm a planeload of terrorists.

Tully refused to go to the hospital until she'd been informed of Jake's situation. Finally, over the police radio they heard that by the time police reinforcements reached the property there were nine men, bound and gagged, awaiting them.

A quick rundown of their identities resulted in multiple arrests for a lengthy list of warrants and parole violations. It seemed the Spiros family business was losing most of its employees at an alarming rate.

Jake was safe and Leonardo's body was being flown back for examination. Tully had given her account of the situation and, after Jake's statement, it would be ruled as an act of self-defense.

Eventually, the station's senior sergeant stepped in and ordered her to the hospital, where her arm was cleaned up and stitched. She refused to stay in overnight and discharged herself as soon as they had finished the dressings, determined to see this horrendous chapter of her life through to the end.

The conversation she had had with Louise before they boarded the helicopter had been recorded and listened to by the task force via Jake's mobile in Tully's pocket. There was nothing Louise could say now that would be able to get her out of this mess.

Tully felt saddened and disturbed. Once she used to think Louise had it all, but in retrospect, without the recognition she felt she deserved, her job had given her nothing.

Surely a person was more than her career?

The thought hit her hard. She could so easily have been another Louise. Her job *had* been her life. Until moving to Townsville, she hadn't spent a weekend out in the sun in years.

The remainder of the night was spent doing paperwork and acting as liaison between two different states of law enforcement. Gratefully she had accepted a new set of clothes from a female constable, replacing the bloodstained, filthy ones she'd been wearing since the day before, but she hadn't been able to contact Jake and had no idea where he was.

She was getting worried. She'd left messages with the station for him to contact her as soon as he reached town, but time was running out.

It was beginning to look like she wouldn't be seeing Jake before she had to leave after all.

* * * *

They booked her on the first flight out that morning back to Melbourne. Accompanying her on the trip would be Louise, complete with her own private police escort. Exhausted, Tully closed her eyes and cradled her injured arm. The painkillers had worn off from the previous night and, determined to stay awake, she had decided not to take any more until Louise had been safely delivered and handed over.

"You look like hell, Chambers."

Tully's eyes snapped open and she found herself looking into Jake's smiling face. Never had a sight been more wonderful.

"Where have you been?" she demanded, torn between relief and frustration, her eyes searching for any damage.

"I got here as soon as I could," he told her calmly. "I'm in one piece," he added with a small grin.

Tully drank in the sight of him greedily as he sat down on the hard plastic chair beside her and took her hand in his. Quickly she filled him in on the outcomes of yesterday's drama.

"It's all over I guess, except for cleaning up a few loose ends and paperwork," she finished with a grimace, and then looked down at their joined hands.

Jake didn't comment immediately, he just idly rubbed one large calloused thumb against the smooth, delicate skin of her hand that he cradled gently.

Her throat seemed to have swollen, making it difficult to swallow as she struggled to hold back a flood of mixed emotions. There was so much she wanted to say to him. How did you even begin to thank someone who was willing to risk their life to save yours?

"It all worked out and you've got what you wanted," Jake said quietly.

"I guess so."

He stared down at their hands still firmly entwined, avoiding her gaze. "You're going back, then?"

The statement made her heart sink to her feet and she felt like curling up in his lap and sobbing her heart out.

"I have to go back to debrief my new boss," she told him, biting the inside of her lip anxiously.

This is what you wanted, came a taunting little voice inside her head. Somehow, though, this wasn't how she'd pictured it when she'd imagined it all finished. Instead of relief, all she felt was...empty, and very, very alone.

Her flight was called over the loudspeaker and the police officer travelling with her, waiting by the departure gate, gave a brief wave to indicate they were ready to board.

Time had run out.

"I'd better get going." Regret echoed loudly in the space between them as she stood, their hands still linked, bringing Jake to his feet as well. "I didn't realize it would be this rushed when it came time to actually leave," she faltered. "I didn't get a chance to thank you, Jake, for everything you did for me." She heard her voice shake and pressed her lips together tightly. "I'll be in touch about the unit in Townsville, let you know what I'll do with the stuff I left there, and—"

"Tully," he interrupted quietly, "is there anything I can do to make you change your mind about going back?" He nodded toward the plane and police officers gathered near a glass door which led to the glaring tarmac outside.

Tully's heart ached. "I have to go back. I need to pick up where I left off or they've won after all. I ran, instead of standing up to them. I won't do that anymore. I have to go back to prove to myself that I still can." Her eyes pleaded with him to understand.

"Detective, we need to get moving," a trim air hostess called, holding a clipboard and pursing her bright red, perfectly painted lips in irritation.

"I'm sorry, Jake, I have to go." Tully reached up and kissed his cheek, then backed away. She felt his grip tighten on her hand before he allowed her to pull away. Walking briskly to the doorway, she didn't look back. Had she turned she would have seen the devastated expression etched across his face as he watched her walk out of his life, helpless to change her mind.

* * * *

The next few weeks were a blur of activity. Tully, protesting loudly, was ordered into protective custody for the weeks leading up to the trial date on the off chance there was any lurking threat still out there. The probability was fairly low considering the majority of Spiros's brawn was either dead or in custody, but the man still had his connections and he was not without the aid of some interstate or overseas sympathizers, so she had twenty-four-hour surveillance and more security than the prime minister.

Jake had pulled some strings of his own. He was not going to let Tully out of his sight for a second, or trust her safety to an unknown factor. She would have protested had she known he was on her detail as well so he remained behind the scenes, watchful and vigilant, a silent sentinel standing guard over the one thing in this world he valued more than life itself.

For two weeks he watched and waited, ready for the slightest sign of trouble. The pain of watching her walk away from him at the airport was something he had never experienced before and never wanted to again. He probably should have just let it go at that if he'd been smart, but he couldn't let her go back to the city, back to face that family at trial by herself. She might think she was tough enough to do it all alone, and maybe she was, but he wasn't about to take any chances with her safety.

His job wasn't over.

There were times, though, like late at night as he sat by the monitor in the room next to hers and watched over her as she slept, that he had to fight the urge to go to her, wrap her tightly in his arms, and take her back to the middle of nowhere where they could hide from the rest of the world and the dangers that seemed to continue to lurk around them.

He wouldn't though. He would do what he'd come here to do and then walk away. Tully had made her decision. He knew she needed time to figure out her future, away from the stress of life on the run. He would wait her out. After all, he'd been trained by the best to do that very thing.

While he waited he would be putting in place his own set of plans that hopefully, one day soon, Tully would want to be a part of.

Chapter Seventeen

Tully pushed through the heavy swinging glass door into her new boss's office without waiting for his secretary to announce her. She charged the superintendent's desk waving a piece of paper before her like a flamenco dancer's fan. "Would you like to explain this to me, Harry?"

"Good morning to you too, Georgia. I hope you know you've upset my new secretary out there," he said dryly.

Tully raised an eyebrow and folded her arms across her chest impatiently. "I'm sure she'll get over it. I, on the other hand, may be a little more difficult to fob off. What the hell is this, Harry? I'm being sent to some hippy commune?"

"It's not a hippy commune." Harry chuckled softly.

"Camp Resilience. What the hell is that?"

"Georgia, take a seat and calm down," he urged, using a fatherly tone he no doubt hadn't used since his own daughters had lived at home.

Tully gritted her teeth but took a deep breath and sat down on the edge of the leather chair.

"I'm recommending you go to this retreat to get help, Georgia. You've been back here for nine months and, quite frankly, I'm worried about you."

"I'm fine, Harry. For goodness sakes, I'm a police officer. It's part of the job. We deal with it and move on. I just want to get on with my life and do my job."

Harry sat across from Tully and watched her closely. "That's just the problem. It's your job that's suffering. I've noticed you seem to be having trouble...connecting with people since you've been back. I also have in my hand the report from the police psychologist who suspects you're suffering from post-traumatic stress disorder." When she flashed daggers at him over that piece of news, he sighed heavily and continued, "This place comes highly recommended. I'm strongly suggesting you go, Georgia." He eyed her with a steely no-nonsense glare that even his most hardened detectives would succumb to.

Tully stared at the man across from her in disbelief. She'd worked with Harry a long time ago, before he'd taken over Louise's job, and had always respected him as a superior, but right now, staring at him, she wasn't sure he was completely rational.

Coming back to work had been a big adjustment, harder than she'd expected if she were to be completely honest. She could also concede it was hard to associate with her colleagues since coming back, but she put this down to having spent too much time alone while she'd been in hiding, something time would remedy.

"I don't need some touchy-feely do-gooder poking around inside my head. I just want to get back to my life."

"That's not going to happen until you deal with this. Look, Georgia, I'm not asking you to do this. Either you check yourself into this place, or I'm going to suspend you until you get help," Harry told her without flinching. Holding Tully's furious stare, he softened his face marginally. "Believe it or not I'm doing this because you're too good a cop to lose. I want the old Georgia back on deck ASAP."

"Well, it's not like I have much of a choice, is it? If those freaks start dancing naked around a campfire singing *Kumbayah*," she muttered, turning on her heel, "I'm outta there."

* * * *

Harry had, bless his meddling, underhanded little heart, organized everything. She was met at the airport and ushered to a connecting flight, and now here she was, stepping out into the arrival lounge of the regional airport she'd been in only one other time.

Katherine Airport.

The last time she was in this place was the day she'd walked away from Jake without a backward glance.

A thud like a stone dropping into a dark, empty pit settled inside her stomach as she wondered, not for the first time, where he was and how he was doing. Of all the stupid places in the country Harry had to send her, why did it have to be up here? There wasn't a "Hippyville" a little closer to a capital city?

Collecting her bag, she sighed wearily as she turned to search for the driver "the place" had sent to pick her up.

She scanned the few faces waiting expectantly for loved ones to appear and for the briefest of moments she thought she was hallucinating when her gaze, pulled like a magnet, met the one gaze she never thought she'd see again.

"Hello, Detective Tully." His deep voice drizzled over her like warm melted chocolate.

"Jake." Her greeting came out sounding strange to her ears, more like a sigh of disbelief than a simple hello. Shaking her head, she wondered if Harry had been right. Were hallucinations a symptom of PTSD? "What are you doing here?" She slipped back into rational detective mode.

"I'm here to pick you up," he said with a shrug.

She blinked up at him in suspicion. "How do you know where I'm going?"

"I know the guy in charge of the place, so I volunteered to come out and get you."

* * * *

Jake had arrived a good forty-five minutes early so he wouldn't miss her. When he saw her walk through the doors of the arrival lounge and head for her luggage, his heart had thumped painfully against his chest and he'd wondered briefly if he might be having some kind of panic attack. She wore a sleek tailored black suit that created an aura of sophistication and confidence around her. Her hair was dark and luscious. Gone was the short, sassy blonde hair she'd worn before. In its place, a carefully sculptured frame of dark hair fell to her shoulders and shimmered as she turned her head.

She looked nothing like the woman he'd lived next door to. For a moment he wondered if he should just turn around and leave her alone. Then as she pushed her sunglasses onto the top of her head and looked around, he caught the briefest flash of uncertainty. It tugged at his heart and made him want to run to her side and hold her tight against him, shield her from the rest of the world and the fears she'd held inside for so long.

He felt the kick in his gut when her eyes clashed with his own, and he waited anxiously for the moment she recognized him, bracing for the possible rejection that might follow.

He'd allowed her the time to make her own decision about their future. He'd used more self-control than he'd ever imagined he possessed to not go running after her at the airport nine months ago. She'd had a lot to sort out and she'd been right to be cautious about their relationship.

He'd used the break to get his own plans sorted out and vowed that when the time came he would make his case once more, this time with more to show and more to offer than before. That time had finally come and he prayed it wasn't all about to blow up in his face.

"I don't know what the hell is going on here, but I'm really tired of being the only one not in on the joke." Her voice quivered with a mix of anger and uncertainty.

"There's no joke, Georgia," he said quietly. "Once we're on the plane I'll explain everything. I promise. Right now we have to get a move on," he said, leaning down to remove the carry bag from her fingers and lead her out the door.

"I just got off a plane. Where on earth are we supposed to go now?" she demanded.

"Just one more leg of the journey, I promise," he told her solemnly.

She followed reluctantly, and they headed for the general aviation area of the airport where a small aircraft sat waiting for them to board. Jake stood aside and allowed her to precede him into the small plane, watching as she took her seat in silence.

It was impossible to hold any form of conversation inside the confines of the small Cessna, and after a while the relentless droning of the engine soon lulled her into an exhausted sleep.

Jake watched Tully as she slept, or rather Georgia. The name seemed to fit the woman beside him perfectly. It sounded confident and assertive, but it didn't suit the woman he'd fallen in love with. Yes, she'd been tough and competent, could handle herself in any number of dangerous situations, but even then, she'd never seemed quite so...untouchable.

She stirred in her sleep and Jake resisted the urge to smooth her hair with his hand. There were dark shadows under her eyes and even in sleep she looked exhausted.

* * * *

Tully awoke with a jolt. She sat up, instantly alert to her surroundings. She couldn't believe she'd fallen asleep. She sent a brief glance toward Jake and saw, much to her discomfort, that he was watching her with that calm, yet observant gaze of his.

"We're about to land."

How many times had she longed to hear that deep, steady voice? Many a night she had tried to remember the sound of it, but her memory had been a poor substitute for the real thing that had had the power to make her insides quiver.

She sent him a terse nod and braced herself for the landing.

When the plane came to a stop, Tully ducked under the doorway and climbed cautiously down the small set of steps to the ground. With a baffled frown, she turned to face Jake and waited for an explanation.

"Welcome to Camp Resilience." He smiled and gestured with his arm to walk toward the cluster of buildings before them.

Tully felt as though she had been winded.

Chapter Eighteen

As she walked toward the farmhouse where she and Jake had stayed, Tully experienced a variety of emotions. Relief, regret, longing, and now, complete and utter confusion. What used to be a run-down old farm was now unbelievably...not.

Six new cabins had been built in a small cluster a few hundred meters from the original farmhouse and through the open doors of the large machinery shed she spotted gym equipment and an indoor spa.

Concrete pathways snaked along between the cabins, gym, and main homestead. They were edged with freshly planted gardens of native grasses and small shrubby bushes. Thick layers of woodchip had been spread around them to retain the almost non-existent moisture the area was famous for and its pungent, earthy smell filled the air.

"I still don't understand." She was unable to take her eyes from the scenery before her.

"Remember I told you I had an idea? Well, this was it. Being out here with you got me thinking about this place. We've been using it for years as somewhere to unwind after deployment.

"To have a place to come to when you need a break, somewhere safe and quiet, made all the difference to a lot of guys who came back from tours with PTSD over the years, myself included. I figured there must be a huge market out here for a place like this."

"You run this place?" Tully asked, turning to face him in surprise.

"I have two psychologists who handle the counselling side of the program, and together we came up with a thirty-day intensive program to treat people with PTSD." His eyes sparkled with barely contained excitement and pride. "Tully, it's huge. This thing has just exploded. We've had so much success within the military that we've now expanded to include a program for regular civilians, everything from burn survivors to victims of violent crimes, and we've considered a separate venture that targets troubled teens. A camp to get kids back on the straight and narrow using a mini-boot camp to give these kids a sense of belonging." Jake stopped, a small self-conscious grin crossing his face. "Sorry, I tend to get a bit carried away when I get started on the subject."

Tully shook her head, feeling dazed. "No...I think it's...fantastic." She looked about her once more and a small uncertain smile tinted her lips. "I think you may have found your niche, Jake Holden," she said softly.

"Who would have thought, huh?" he agreed, his eyes moving over her face, searching for something she wasn't sure she wanted him to find.

"It still doesn't explain why I'm here," she said, breaking the silence and taking a small step back.

He seemed to ignore her question. Asking instead, "Was going back to your life everything you thought it would be?" Although his question seemed casual enough, she didn't miss the underlying tension he tried to hide.

She gave a small scowl. "It's taking a bit to settle back in again, but I'm doing okay."

"No panic attacks, night sweats, insomnia?" he prodded.

She squirmed. "Nothing I can't handle."

"Tully, believe it or not, you're not handling it as well as you think you are. I've talked to your boss. I know that on more than one occasion you've displayed a reckless disregard for your own safety in the line of duty," he quoted gravely, indicating he'd also, somehow, read the reports written on her and the disciplinary action she had been threatened with since her return to work.

"That's none of your business, and if I felt a need to explain myself to you, I would, but I don't, so let's just drop it," she told him, gritting her teeth angrily.

"Your boss made it my business to make sure you were given help and until we give him the all clear on you, you won't be going back to work." He waited until that sank in before continuing, the hard edge dropping. "If you don't acknowledge and deal with this problem, at best you'll lose your job, at worst you'll get yourself killed. I want to help you, Tully."

"Do you, Jake? Really?" she challenged him, her voice low with quiet fury. "I seem to remember how my career was always the one big stumbling block in the way of our relationship. Wouldn't it make it so much simpler if you never recommended I was fit to return to duty? How do I know you'll be impartial?"

"Because I'm not the psychologist and that's the only person you have to impress." Jake shrugged. "You're here because you need to deal with your condition before something happens to you," Jake told her firmly, "and don't say you're handling it because you're not."

"I'm here because my boss ordered me to come. I just want to get it over and done with." That cool, untouchable shield had been pulled, firmly, back into place.

"You have to want to get better, Tull—Georgia." Jake stumbled on her name but amended his error quickly.

"Tully." Her voice sounded stilted as she corrected him. "I prefer Tully."

"Me too," he said, then added over his shoulder as he turned away, "Who knows? Maybe we'll find her again in there somewhere."

* * * *

"So, how's it going?" Jake asked Tully as she neared the front of the homestead after her usual evening run, two weeks into her program.

Tully took a minute to catch her breath. She'd slowed to a walk, cooling down, before looking up at him. "It hasn't been too horrible," she admitted.

"Well, don't go overboard on the praise."

Tully allowed a small smile to escape. It was so much better than not too horrible. It was actually a relief. She'd had no idea what was awaiting her at the beginning of the program but it was nothing like she'd been half expecting. There were no warm fuzzy group hugs, no holding hands and chanting, nothing even slightly weird, just people talking and getting a lot of things off their chests.

"It's been…enlightening," she relented as he fell into step beside her. They walked for a while in silence until Tully stopped and put her hand on Jake's arm lightly.

"Jake, I want to thank you. You persisted with me, even when I wasn't exactly appreciative of your attempts." She allowed a small smile when he raised an eyebrow at her understatement. "I'm sorry I was so thickheaded when all you were trying to do was help."

Jake's smile crept into his eyes as he looked down at her thoughtfully. "I do believe, Miss Tully, you're on the road to recovery."

"I do believe you're right." She smiled up at him, warmly and genuinely.

He studied her for a minute before he reached a decision. "You know, after you've finished your program I want to talk to you about a job offer," Jake said so quietly that at first Tully wasn't sure she'd heard him properly.

"I already have a job, Jake, and I'm not into the whole psychologist thing," she said warily.

"I want to expand this program, Tully. I told you about the troubled teens retreat I'm working on? Well, I also want to include a fitness program and self-defense class. You'd be perfect for it. To the kids in particular you would be a fantastic role model, Tully. You speak their language. You know the streets and the pitfalls where a lot of kids lose their way. What better person to show them they can turn their lives around?"

Tully's gaze focused on the horizon as she listened to his argument. Much to her surprise, she didn't immediately dismiss the idea.

"It's just something to think about. There's no pressure, Tully, no strings. I just want you to know you have another option."

Jake left her staring after him as he jogged back to the homestead. Tully followed at a slower pace, realizing she was indeed thinking about his offer. It was the knowledge that it didn't absolutely petrify her to think of such a drastic change that seemed to flabbergast her the most.

* * * *

It was almost miraculous, Tully thought upon completion of her last class two weeks later, the difference thirty days could make in a person's life. Who would notice a difference in her? she wondered disconcertingly. Her boss and her workmates she supposed, but would they? She wasn't close to any of them, not since Spence, and she wasn't sure she even wanted to be.

What did she have to go back to after here? She had no pets, didn't even own a plant. What kind of emotionally retarded human being couldn't bring themselves to at least own a plant?

Something had been missing for a long time now with her work. Yes, she loved it but even before the whole Spiros debacle she'd felt as though she wanted to be doing more. Not just solving crimes, as important as that was. She wanted to do something to prevent crimes, to save victims before they became victims.

Jake's teenage retreat fanned a flame of possibilities inside her. Maybe she *could* reach the troubled teens before they lost their souls to the streets and became unreachable, before they became the next criminals she was forced to throw in jail to waste their lives.

Would that be enough for her? Could it be a new path to try? Should she take the risk? The endless possibilities and arguments had swirled in her head for two weeks now.

Jake and Lachlan, the psychologist she'd been working with, had sat down with her earlier in the day and shown her their proposal for the program. She'd quizzed them on endless details, all of which they had well-thought-out and suitable solutions for. It seemed like an amazing project and one that could be hers for the taking if she were just brave enough to make the leap.

However, therein lay the problem. She had no clue how Jake felt about her anymore. He was still attracted to her, that much she knew, but could they sustain a relationship out here and survive? What if it didn't work? They'd be stuck out here together, forced to endure an uncomfortable working relationship. Could she really gamble on her future like that?

Her last day finally arrived and Tully was still no closer to making a decision. With a heavy heart she went into Jake's office and faced him across his desk.

"You're turning me down?" he asked before she could even open her mouth. His disappointment was painfully clear.

"I can't make up my mind here. This place makes everything... distorted. I need to go back home and think about it rationally," she told him, searching his eyes for understanding.

Jake sighed, holding her gaze steadily. "Okay, Tully. Do what you have to do."

Tully hesitated, frowning. "It's just that, I don't know if we can work together...out here. I mean, we have a past and it might get in the way."

"Would it?" Jake asked, his voice in that annoyingly neutral tone.

"I feel like I haven't had any control over my life for so long, especially lately. I just want to make up my own mind," she explained, trying to hold his gaze but finding it hard to look at him and speak at the same time.

"Then go and make up your mind, Tully. I want you to be happy. I won't lie. I want you to be happy here, with me, but I don't want you to wonder if you made the right decision. Go back to the city and think about it. Your job will still be waiting for you," he said softly.

"What about you, Jake? Will you be here waiting too?" she asked, almost fearful of his answer.

"I'll be right here waiting like I have been from the start, Tully. I've been waiting my whole life for you. Another few weeks won't matter," he told her, holding her gaze with a tenderness so potent she almost sobbed with relief.

Outside the engine of the plane whined to life and Tully saw people begin to file out toward the aircraft to board.

Tears filled her eyes. Why did it always come down to her walking away from everything that meant something to her? Tully squeezed her eyes shut before taking a shaky breath. "I guess it's time to go. Thank you for everything, Jake. I'm sorry I was such a pain in the butt for the majority of the time I was here. I'm glad you never gave up on me though."

"That's the one thing I will never do, Tully," he promised, standing and walking toward her.

He stood close enough that she could smell the warm, clean scent of him and her fingers itched to reach out to him. Instead she leaned forward and kissed his lips lightly, closing her eyes as she pulled back and fought for control of her wayward emotions.

"Good-bye, Jake."

He didn't reply and Tully realized he was fighting his own battle, trying to remain impartial to her decision to leave.

She felt his eyes on her as she walked toward the plane and with every step she felt her heart break a little more. *This wasn't the way it was supposed to end.*

Her steps faltered as the statement echoed inside her head.

Why did she need to fight the inevitable? Yes, lately all the decisions in her life had resulted from the actions of others. She'd had to give up her life because of the Spiros trial. Yes, she had been angry that Jake and her boss had conspired against her to force her into treatment, but hadn't that been the best thing that could have happened? Hadn't coming here forced her to deal with the things she'd been pushing away because they were simply too hard to face alone?

Was going away to think about Jake's offer really something she needed to do? Didn't she already know in her heart that being a part of this new program would be exactly the thing she wanted to do to make a difference?

Jake hadn't manipulated her. He had simply made her a job offer. Tully stopped as she reached the steps of the plane and the pilot held out his hand for her overnight bag.

* * * *

Jake watched her walk across the clearing toward the plane but as she reached the stairs he had to turn away. He couldn't do this a second time, watch her board a plane that would fly her out of his life again. He simply wasn't strong enough to do it. He walked back inside and stood in the kitchen, arms braced against the sink, head lowered, and closed his eyes as the plane taxied away, preparing to take off.

Would she come back? He'd told her he'd wait and he would, but what he didn't tell her was that every damn second of the wait would just about kill him. He didn't want to face the possibility she wouldn't be back. He just couldn't. The plane picked up speed and he heard it gather momentum and lift into the air taking his life away. He forced himself to take a breath but it physically hurt to do so and he wondered if a broken heart could, in fact, kill a person. The back door creaked and he cursed the intrusion into his private agony.

Drawing in a breath and forcing his face into a mask of indifference, he turned and felt as though someone had punched him in his stomach.

For a long time they simply stood and faced each other, neither quite sure what to say.

"What's wrong, Tully? What happened?" he finally asked, his voice coming out raw and husky.

"I realized something as I was getting on the plane."

He stared at her, too scared to wonder if it had been good or bad.

"I realized it wasn't the job I wanted."

His heart dropped to his feet. This was it then, he thought dismally. "We can talk about it. You can tell me what you want—"

She stopped him mid-sentence with a small smile.

"The job is amazing. It's exactly what I want to do, but it's not what I want to stay for." When he looked at her in confused defeat she explained quickly. "I don't want to walk away from *you,* Jake. I'd managed to alienate just about everyone in my life before I met you. I was so convinced I was tough enough to handle everything alone that's how I ended up. Until you. You just don't give up," she said in exasperation.

Jake smiled.

"It's not this place that makes everything seem possible, it's *you.* I can go back to my life and be okay, but I want more than that, I want to feel the way I feel when I'm with you. I don't care where that is, as long as you're there. I can't walk away from you again, Jake," she whispered as her voice broke.

Jake crossed the room and gathered her roughly into his arms and held her, unable to speak in case his own voice quivered unsteadily.

Tully pulled back after a while and smiled. "Does this mean the job's mine?"

Jake chuckled as he searched her face. "The job, me, this place, you get it all, Tully. It's a package deal," he said, only half joking.

"I love you, Jake. I'm absolutely terrified, but I know it's going to be okay."

"Tully, I've loved you since the minute you tossed me over your head like a miniature female Hulk Hogan. We're going to be better than okay. With your brawn and my brains, we can handle anything life throws at us."

She beamed, and he kissed her long and hard, loving the feel of her in his arms once more.

He knew this stubborn, sexy, *infuriating* woman would challenge his patience, argue, and aggravate him just as she had since day one—but he wouldn't want it any other way—after all, Go Hard or Go Home had been his unit's motto.

It was going to be one hell of a ride and Jake couldn't wait to start.

About the Author:

Karlene lives on the beautiful Mid North Coast of NSW in Australia. She's a mum to four beautiful children and is grateful to have a loving and patient husband who no longer thinks it's strange that she talks to fictional characters throughout the day!

You can find more information about Karlene and her other books at http:// karlybm.webs.com as well as on Face Book.

More Books by Karlene Blakemore-Mowle:
The Cattleman's Runaway Bride
Operation Summer Storm

Also by Karlene Blakemore-Mowle:

Operation Summer Storm
by Karlene Blakemore-Mowle

eBook ISBN: 9781615725861
Print ISBN: 9781615725878

Romance Suspense
Novel of 67,404 words

Tate Maddox is on the run and running out of time. Summer Sheldon has the evidence to clear his name—but it comes at a price. Summer's sister has been kidnapped and Tate must go on one last mission to rescue her—or the evidence disappears...along with his last chance at freedom.

There's only one way for either of them to get what they want and that is to work together, but how can he trust a blackmailer? How far will she go to save the only family she has left?

Forgotten Memories
by Suzanne Brandyn

eBook ISBN: 9781615726462
Print ISBN: 9781615726479

Romance Suspense
Novel of 70,694 words

It's easy to forget, but much harder to remember.

Following the death of Catherine Berg's father, a car accident leaves her with amnesia. Catherine needs to find her memories to escape the shell of a woman she has become. Not having a past, she is struggling with the present.

Nathan Alexander a lawyer and pilot almost collides with Catherine when he attempts to make touchdown on Port Macquarie's airstrip. Her attitude surprises him, as they were childhood sweethearts. Nathan announces he has arrived to claim his half inheritance of her father's company, Macquarie Airways, instead he claims her heart.

When he learns of her amnesia, he is determined to help her remember not only him, but also her past. Nathan is on a flight back to Port Macquarie from the outback. His aircraft disappears. Search and Rescue fail to locate him.

Catherine has lost one man she loved, she isn't about to lose another. She has to find the courage to climb back into an aircraft to rescue the man she loves from the mountainous ranges of Outback Australia.

Eternal Press

Official Website:
www.eternalpress.biz

Blog:
http://eternalpressauthors.blogspot.com/

Reader Chat Group:
http://groups.yahoo.com/group/EternalPressReaders

MySpace:
http://www.myspace.com/eternalpress

Twitter:
http://twitter.com/EternalPress

Facebook:
http://www.facebook.com/profile.php?id=1364272754

Google +:
https://plus.google.com/u/0/115524941844122973800

Good Reads:
http://www.goodreads.com/profile/EternalPress

Shelfari:
http://www.shelfari.com/eternalpress

Library Thing:
http://www.librarything.com/catalog/EternalPress

We invite you to drop in, visit with our authors and stay in touch
for the latest news, releases and more!

Printed in Australia
AUOC010806180412
251962AU00001B/1/P